Tales from Comanche County:
The Peculiar Education of Max Freeman

Max Yoho

Dancing Goat Press
Topeka, Kansas

Tales from Comanche County
The Peculiar Education of Max Freeman

For Information address: Dancing Goat Press
3013 SW Quail Creek Dr., Topeka, Kansas 66614

PRINTING HISTORY
First Printing, Dec. 2001
ISBN 0-9708160-1-4

Publisher's Cataloging-in-Publication

Yoho, Max,
    Tales from Comanche County : the peculair education
of Max Freeman / Max Yoho. – 1st ed.
    p. cm.
    ISBN 0-9708160-1-4

    1. Comanche County (Kans.)--Fiction.   I. Title.

PS3575.035T35 2001   813'.6
                            QB133-8

PRINTED IN THE UNITED STATE OF AMERICA
BY HALL COMMERCIAL PRINTING, TOPEKA, KANSAS

"…on the seventh day, while resting, God again observed His handiwork and He was pleased—

—then he noticed Oklahoma."

From the Book of *Provocations*
as remembered by Jack Freeman,
Comanche County rancher

For Carol, who knows how to cut through the gristle and get to the gravy.   ·

With special thanks to

Joy Thompson
Debra Jenkins
Nancy and Bob Keith
Naomi Patterson

Contents

Tales From Comanche Country
The Peculiar Education of Max Freeman
by
Max Yoho

Prologue

I am old. My hip bones are no longer my friends. My knees? Unreliable as a landlord's promise. I most often wear Uncle Jack's bequeathed, smooth, well oiled .45 Smith and Wesson revolver which is nearly as old as God, so not many folks seem to choose to give me trouble.

Dang good thinking!

My father told me that when I was three minutes old, I raised up on my elbows and took a good look at the world. He did not mention whether or not the world pleased me, and I don't remember. I was strong, and he pegged me for a prize fighter. I was named after Max Baer, the boxer, but boxing was not my bent. History was my bent.

I was denied the advanced degree in history for which I

was so well qualified. The cushy "Head of the History Department" position, in which I intended to have a long and prestigious career, was never offered me. Certain professors in a certain Kansas institution of *higher* learning were too hide-bound, too set in mental concrete, to accept the fact that the last wound of the Civil War occurred in 1902. They could not accept the fact that there existed a fossilized mud turtle with what appeared to be a fossilized celluloid collar button in its belly, even though I offered to prove it by tying a rope around them and lowering them into the well. They also could not accept the fact that during the Great Albanian Potato Rebellion, thousands of Albanians died, dropping like flies, because they found starvation preferable to eating Idahos, and would sooner see their grandmas skinned and boiled than eat a russet. Some of my professors seemed to be in denial, and declared there had never even been an Albanian Potato Rebellion.

"Ludicrous," they told me.

"Bull hockey," I told them. "I know what I know."

My life in academia ended abruptly.

1

Raiders and Marauders

Large chunks of my long childhood summers were spent in Comanche County, Kansas—maybe learning more there each summer than I learned in a winter's worth of school. It was a long time ago, and the stories I heard were sometimes dolloped out to me in bits and pieces. In the early hearings, I was not much more than nothing. Still, I can remember most of what they told me. Words rattle in my head like rawhide snares on a Battle of the Wilderness drum.

Early on, my great Uncle Jack Freeman, my great Aunt Tildy, and I were sitting on the front porch because, even though Uncle Jack always intended to build a back porch, he never got around to it. He was simply too busy dealing with a cannon ball bruise to his ankle, the Albanian potato difficulties, and the Emperor of China.

Evening was the time for rocking and pondering. Uncle Jack and Aunt Tildy mostly rocked, and I mostly pondered a fresh pitcher of lemonade.

"You ought to tell Max about the time the four raiders came through," Aunt Tildy told Uncle Jack.

"For the benefit of accuracy," Uncle Jack corrected, "they were not 'raiders' in the classical sense of the word. They were 'marauders.' Raiders never travel in groups of less than five, although they often exceed that number."

"Well, then," Aunt Tildy probed, "in the classical sense of the word, how many does it take to piece together the amount required to maraud?"

Uncle Jack pulled out his sharper-than-any-need-to-be knife and stropped it across the upper part, the rougher part, of his higher-than-a-snake-can-usually-bite boot.

"Judas Priest," he pointed out. "It is apparent that when God created Eve from the rib of Adam, he did not include any portion of the small nodule just behind the pancreas which enables one to tell the difference between raiders and marauders. It is far more complex than just a matter of numbers. Sometimes raiders maraud and sometimes marauders raid."

Maybe because the time was creeping toward bedtime, Aunt Tildy said, "Jack, you ought to tell Max about the time the four raiding marauders came here marauding and raiding."

Uncle Jack shot me a long-suffering look which told me that it did not take a firecracker scientist to predict the futility of trying to explain some things to a woman.

But I could tell a delicate balance had been reached between them. Uncle Jack tried again, "There were four of them."

Aunt Tildy grinned and interrupted, "They were from Nebraska!"

"For Christ's sweet sake, Tildy, raiders and marauders do *not* come from Nebraska. They came from…well, Perdition, if you must have a place."

As if I needed to reinforce my reputation for dumbness, I asked, "Well, where, in relationship to Nebraska, is Perdition?"

The sadness of Uncle Jack's eyes seemed to move slowly down his long, bumpy nose and head in my direction. It lit on my cheeks, turning them pink. I knew I had disappointed him again.

"Perdition," he told me, fully convinced that I was carrying in my veins a dangerously high level of Oklahoma blood, "precisely matches the longitudinal and latitudinal coordinates of Oklahoma."

Aunt Tildy cooled herself with a Palmetto leaf fan which she had inadvertently slipped under her jacket at Ida Brown's funeral, because Ida Brown had once mentioned that Aunt Tildy's gooseberry pie was, perhaps, a tad too tart. But now Ida Brown lay amoldering in her grave with a sour expression on her face while Aunt Tildy sipped sweet lemonade and cooled herself with a Palmetto leaf fan which she had inadvertently slipped under her jacket at Ida Brown's funeral.

"They just seemed to appear out of nowhere." Uncle Jack mused. "Out of the west, with the sun at their backs. On golden stallions they came, wearing long, snow-white dusters, and each, crosswise over his breast, wore a bandoleer filled with .45-70 cartridges. I told your Aunt Tildy to fetch the rifle and she…"

"Bull hockey!" Aunt Tildy intercepted. "They came in an old Ford with the radiator steaming, and yes, they were white, and yes, they were dusty, and, conceivably, they might have had 45¢ or 70¢ between them."

"In the name of all that is holy, Tildy, I am not telling about when Bonnie and Clyde came through raiding and marauding, I am telling about when those ruffians on the golden stallions…"

But Aunt Tildy cautioned him with a movement of the Palmetto leaf fan which Ida Brown had, in all likelihood personally used, but did not currently (in so far as we know) require, and announced that there had, most likely, been enough raiding and marauding for one night. She said it was time for me to go to bed, and she told me that if I needed to go outside in the night, then I should *go* outside. She reminded me that I was in Comanche County now, and that by and large and for the most part, boys in Comanche County did *not* pee through the screen door. I will insert here, for the benefit of any "Aunt Tildys" who may still exist, that in the dark of night, a screen door, no matter how rusted and thin, is a welcome protection for a boy when the coyotes are howling and the owls are hooting with goodness knows what in mind.

2

Jack and Tildy

"Godamighty!" biscuits were invented by my Great Aunt Tildy in 1902. The predominant ingredient was cockleburs which, with the exception of rattlesnakes, was the Freeman's most abundant crop. My Great Uncle Jack had named them with his first bite. When Aunt Tildy admonished him for his blasphemy, Uncle Jack quoted Revelations 1:8: "I am Alpha and Omega, the beginning and the ending."

"To put that another way," Uncle Jack continued, "These biscuits are Godamighty stickery going in, and they will, undoubtedly, be Godamighty stickery going out. Just read your Bible, woman!"

Uncle Jack spoke just strongly enough to maintain his position as head of the household, but just mildly enough to acknowledge that he was not yet completely out of the doghouse because of the haystack episode and especially because of the baseball game.

Tall, lean and sun-ripened, Uncle Jack sported a heavy, drooping mustache which would have bowed the neck of a lesser man, and always wore tall, earth-ripened boots. He embraced the Kansas state motto, *"Ad Astra Per Aspera,"* (To the Stars Through Difficulties) and, if he found more *"Aspera"* in life than *"Astra,"* he accepted that with good humor as a fact of life.

Aunt Tildy looked like a wren that had been too long on a skinny-worm diet. She was a bony bundle of peppery love. Her patience with my Great Uncle Jack might have given her a good shot at sainthood, but Aunt Tildy did not have much patience with saints. "Saints think they are just a little bit better than the rest of us," she often said. And you better not ever bring up the subject of angels dancing on the heads of pins around Aunt Tildy! "Them angels ought to have had a few goats to care for to take their minds off such foolishness," she would tell you.

Their ranch lay south, in that rough border area of Comanche County, Kansas. It abutted the Oklahoma Territory, cheek-to-cheek and jowl-to-jowl. Or, as Uncle Jack would have corrected, "If it abutted, then say what you mean! It was not cheek-to-cheek, nor was it jowl-to-jowl. It was pure and simply butt-to-butt."

Uncle Jack claimed they were "clear out where the hoot owls were forced by loneliness to make goo-goo eyes at the chickens." But I did not observe that behavior for myself, and I did not include it later in my master's thesis.

Uncle Jack also declared that his ranch was the sacred and hereditary home of the little massasauga rattlesnake. He said they came there to be born, and they came back to die. I had no reason to doubt it, except it seemed to me that most of them never bothered to leave.

With him, as with many of his neighbors, it was just common sense to place the outhouse on the Oklahoma side of the state border. Not an inch of Oklahoma belonged to Great Uncle Jack, but without a hint of a grin, he called it "squatters rights." Uncle Jack maintained that God created Oklahoma for the sanitary requirements of the Great State of Kansas.

Now, as Uncle Jack told it, life in those days was mostly pretty hard. "Sometimes it was so hot and dry that almost nothing grew. Praying for rain was about all the excitement we had. Well, one June I stomped eighteen rattlesnakes to death, but the joy of that soon palled. In July I tied the tails of two cats together and suspended them 'in the interim' as one might say, over the clothesline and enjoyed that spectacle until Tildy came out with a pair of scissors and performed an act of benevolence which left one cat with mostly two tails and one cat with mostly no tail. Then she proceeded to lecture *me* about the evils of being cruel to God's creatures! Judas Priest!"

Uncle Jack rocked in his old chair and mused and pondered. He scratched himself deeply, satisfyingly, and disgustingly. Aunt Tildy's neck bone popped from habit as she averted her eyes.

3

An Invasion

"It was about the middle of August, 1902 when the ball-game manifested itself," Uncle Jack explained.

Uncle Jack maintained that the game happening at all was a pure act of God. Aunt Tildy counter-maintained that what with all the people in China, Persia and Birmingham, Alabama to watch over, it seemed a miracle that God could find the time to organize a baseball game. Uncle Jack pondered that thought and concluded she was most probably correct. "It was likely old Satan who caused that game," he decided. He shook his head in sad disappointment and added, "And after all I've done for him!"

As Uncle Jack explained it, his haystack became a little

bit on fire as a result of a conflict between the wind and his briar pipe. As he tried to beat out the fire with a wetted blanket, he inadvertently sent a smoke signal which challenged any or all Oklahomans to compete in a baseball game to prove, once and for all, whether the Oklahoma Territory, or the Great State of Kansas contained God's chosen people.

According to Uncle Jack, no one was more surprised than he when, a few days later, a ball team from Oklahoma broke the serenity of the horizon and approached like a storm containing strong winds and a possibility of hail. Aunt Tildy, who was in the backyard boiling soap, viewed their arrival without a flinch or a murmur. Like the cockleburs, the rattlesnakes, the grasshoppers, the cockroaches, and the eternally-blowing red dust, an infestation of Oklahomans was just one more pestilence the Good Lord had seen fit to add to the weight on her patient, bony shoulders.

They arrived, some on ponies, one on a Texas Longhorn steer. The team's pitcher came afoot, juggling three nine-pound cannon balls which Uncle Jack, without a shred of knowledge of their provenance, pronounced to be from the Battle of the Wilderness.

The hair growing out of this fellow's ears was braided, but Uncle Jack stressed that "They were not overly long braids, nor were they plaited in any particular style which might be considered in any way elegant."

Obviously pleased and satisfied with his description of the pitcher's ear hair, Uncle Jack paused and pondered how best to describe the Oklahoma team as a whole: "Scraggly! Flea-ridden—Scruffy! They appeared to be a misbegotten union of buffalo, coyotes and porcupines. An amalgamation." He sucked and savored that word. "Yes, an amalgamation of the worst of society—the dregs, the mud from the bottom of a nearly dry water hole. If God had had any compassion for mothers, he would have let the dams of those whelps die in childbirth before they had a chance to understand what evil they had unleashed."

Uncle Jack's green eyes squinted tightly as he searched for a succinct summation. "That team was about as near to an average cross-section of Oklahomans as you might ever hope to find.

"Behind the Oklahoma ball team," Uncle Jack expanded, "rolled, meandered and flounced what would now most likely be called a 'cheering section.' They appeared to be mostly female, with a good deal of human blood in some of them. From time to time, with no signal apparent to the eye, they would twirl their skirts, display their massive thighs and holler, 'Eat 'em, Eat 'em, Raw, Raw, Raw!'"

Aunt Tildy rocked and pondered. "I have not previously heard you mention anything about 'massive thighs,'" she said.

After four matches, Uncle Jack's pipe still was not drawing properly and still was not performing in such a manner as to comfort his soul.

"Dang, I meant to tell you! Over in Coldwater the other day I got to talking to old Tige Semple. We were reminiscing about the ballgame, and he surprised me by saying that the Oklahoma cheering section had massive thighs."

"Bull hockey!" Aunt Tildy's face saddened. "And in front of the boy!"

Uncle Jack failed with his last match and grumbled, "It's not my fault if they had massive thighs."

Great Uncle Jack had no hobby in the traditional sense. He did not walk the fields collecting arrowheads, nor did he commit passages of Dickens to memory. But it seemed to me that he was a pretty good authority on the Bible, though, because he could use scripture to prove what might seem almost unprovable. In later years I learned that most of his quotes came from his sort-of step-father, Lincoln Coosey, who had a penchant when quoting scripture for erring on the side of the sinners.

If Uncle Jack had one passion, it was to define and explain the Oklahoman. And he would have been the first to admit that this was a heavy burden to lug around. Uncle Jack firmly believed Oklahomans were a lost tribe of Israel, but he seemed to hold no particular grudge against God for bungling the job of losing them. Aunt Tildy said Uncle Jack had more patience with God than might be reasonably expected. But, on my own recognizance, I will state my belief that God may have bent over backwards for Uncle Jack a few times too.

Anyway, Uncle Jack said that the Oklahoma ball team dismounted, "belching and making other disgusting noises," and explained the purpose of their visit.

Uncle Jack did his best to subjugate his enthusiasm at having a "go" at Oklahomans, and set about to assemble a Kansas team capable of "defeating, demoralizing, and possibly eviscerating the enemy." He put his son, Art, on a pony and told him to ride like Paul Revere to the neighbors. "Tell them the Oklahomans have arrived and to come immediately! Tell them this is a pure and simple case of *Ad Astra Per Aspera!*"

The neighbors appeared more quickly than would seem possible. They came, unaware of the impending baseball game. They came because Art, a slow lad at best (and lacking his father's education or way with words) had ridden through shouting "Come quick! The Oklahomans has arove, and it's a simple case of *Dad's ass is in plaster!*"

It took a while to get things sorted out, and some of the neighbors grumbled. Uncle Jack, always a sensitive host, apologized for his lack of forethought in laying in an adequate supply of plaster, and then segued smoothly into the subject of baseball.

The Kansans and the Oklahomans settled in, regarding each other with a safe distance between. I once asked Uncle Jack how, since the Kansans and the Oklahomans were all just poor, simple country people with little money to spend on apparel, had they been somehow stirred and moiled together, would anyone be able to tell them apart? He looked down his long, humpy nose with obvious disappointment in me. "Son," he said, "The Lord doth put a difference between the Egyptians and Israel. Exodus 11:7." That answer seemed to please him grandly, even though I didn't see how it answered my question. The sadness in his eyes told me it pained him to learn I could not be depended on to differentiate between Kansans and Oklahomans. The sadness in his eyes told me he was now convinced that someday I would probably live in Tulsa or Stillwater—by choice.

The sun was slanting low and hot across the front porch, but it didn't bother Uncle Jack's story telling. He was laughing, remembering. He said that on that August day it was a mighty-surprised Tildy who welcomed her neighbors as they came pouring in. She soon excused herself to mind the soap kettle which, hanging from a tripod, burbled over a bed of hot, glowing embers.

It was at about this point Uncle Jack noticed one of the Oklahomans casting, with difficulty, an eye which, left to its own proclivity and natural inclination, would have looked toward Macon, Georgia—but looked instead at Aunt Tildy. Aunt Tildy stirred the soap, maybe aware and maybe not, of the Oklahoman. The fellow began moving, persevering, somewhat sideways, but ever in the general direction of the soap kettle. As he got closer, Aunt Tildy, doubtlessly feeling a presence of evil, scooted for the house. As soon as she was gone, that old boy picked up the soap paddle and started licking it with a fervor seldom witnessed this side of Paradise.

By this time Uncle Jack had eased out his sharp-honed knife preparatory to changing the Oklahoman's lifestyle, appearance, and ability to reproduce, but the fellow made a sign for a parley. He licked that soap paddle again, and his eyes rolled up toward heaven. "Mister," he said, "that's some of the finest eaten' I've ever had. I'll trade you thirteen ponies for your woman who cooks so fine." Uncle Jack shook the man's hand warmly and said that was the best offer he ever had, and he only regretted he could not afford to feed thirteen ponies. The Oklahoman, in a burst of magnamosity rarely encountered on the border, lowered his bid to nine ponies.

Uncle Jack thanked him again, but was forced to admit he still couldn't afford the trade. Plainly embarrassed for Uncle Jack, the Oklahoman stirred his toe in the red dirt and blurted, "All right, dang it, two ponies, and that's the worst I can do."

Uncle Jack put his hand on the fellow's shoulder and let his gaze follow along in the general direction of Macon, Georgia.

"It's a pure bitch of a situation," he told him, "but the truth is, I simply can't afford to be rich." He encouraged another lick of the soap paddle, and added with all the modesty he could muster, "Everything Tildy cooks tastes that good or nearly that good."

I watched as Aunt Tildy rocked and pondered, unsure if she had been complimented or insulted. "Get on with the baseball story," she said.

4

The Rules of the Game

The makeup of the Oklahoma team, Uncle Jack took pains to point out, was worthy of contemplation. First of all, they called their team the *"Red Sock,"* because one of the members did, indeed, own a red sock. It was an object of pride with them, and they regarded it as an icon of civilization. It was a symbol of the cultural standing they dreamed of someday achieving. And, "God bless those Oklahomans," Uncle Jack sighed, "they are still trying."

Most of the team members were young scamps, but some of the older men had fought on either side in the Civil War. There were even a few Indians.

Uncle Jack explained to me that the men who had

fought for the North called it "The War to Put Down Secession." The men who fought for the South called it "The War Against Northern Aggression." The Indians, seeing the palefaces killing each other hand-over-fist, called it "the funniest damn thing they had ever seen."

Uncle Jack said that the official rules of baseball had not yet reached the Oklahomans, so they explained their position: all twelve of them would be allowed to play at the same time or they would destroy all of southern Kansas, the fields would be burned and covered with salt, the calves and lambs would be slaughtered, and the progeny of the Kansas team would be cursed with boils and leprosy unto the fourth generation.

Uncle Jack had no problem with that; it was about what one might expect. The whole parley went, in fact, more smoothly than most negotiations with Oklahomans. He was able to modify and weaken the clause which gave the winning team the right to disembowel and dismember the losing team. Uncle Jack always seemed to sit a little straighter, look a little more noble, when he explained that no matter how much the Oklahomans stomped and no matter how much the Oklahomans swore, he had stood four-square *against* the winning pitcher being allowed to eat the raw liver of the losing pitcher.

One time, as Uncle Jack repeated and honed this part of the story, Aunt Tildy, who had heard it enough and more than enough, said, "I just happen to like liver!"

"My sweet patooti! Tildy, I doubt you would like *raw, human* liver!"

"Well," Aunt Tildy mulled, "men are the most exasperating of the species, and have no idea at all as to what a woman might like."

The ballgame would be played in Ebbets' Field, called that for the plain and simple reason that it belonged to old One-eyed Charlie Ebbets. The field abutted Uncle Jack's claim, and was just a few yards from the back door of Jack and Tildy's cabin. Charlie also volunteered to be umpire, and all agreed to that. The reason was this: the image of justice is usually portrayed as blindfolded, and since a baseball game is more important than your usual justice, an umpire with one good eye would balance out about right.

The Kansas team, being at a decided disadvantage with only five players, would be allowed to tie rattlesnakes at first and third bases as basemen. For part of the outfield, the Kansas team found three armadillos who were hungry and surly and seemed to have an inherent dislike for Oklahomans. Daughters of the Kansas team, girls under the age of nine (and there seemed to be many of them) would be allowed to fire small-bore rifles at any Oklahoman between third base and home plate. But—and the Oklahomans were adamant about this—those girls, those many-hued girls, those girls (freckled, red of hair), those girls (with wondrous, radiant black hair which changed color at the whim of the sun), those girls (whose hair was so lovingly blond as to make a Norwegian saint gnash her teeth in envy and anger and hurl lutefisk at the crucifix), those girls could only shoot between the knee and the ankle.

As the two teams assembled on the field, Uncle Jack announced that the Kansas team wanted to start the game with a prayer. The Oklahoma team quickly went into a huddle and then declared that the Kansans could make a choice: they could have God on their side, or the rattlesnake at third base—not both.

Uncle Jack, as captain of the Kansas team, told me

he had let his eyes meander over the Oklahoma team and concluded that, as a general rule, one could not do much better than God. But, since they were dealing with Oklahomans, the rattlesnake seemed the more prudent choice.

The batting order was determined in this manner: the captains of each team would take each other's thumbs into their mouths and would bite until one (the loser) cried "calf-rope." Uncle Jack said when that Oklahoma captain's thumb came under his nose—that ragged, broken thumbnail, that thumbnail under which lay the frosting of all the sins of mankind and at least the southern part of Tulsa—he began to have grave fears and misapprehensions. He said something in his mind flashed to Exodus 29:20, but he couldn't quite remember. "It was something about the thumb. Yes! '...upon the thumb of their right hand and up...'" but he could not for the life of him remember "up" what.

Uncle Jack declared that the lessons we learn at our mothers' knees are blessed, and he was eternally grateful his mother had taught him the rudiments of manners. "No, sir," he told that Oklahoma captain, "You folks are our guests. You go ahead and bat first. Hell, I'd rather have a ruptured kidney than bite your thumb."

The Oklahoman had Uncle Jack's thumb already in his mouth. Not wanting to waste it, he graciously acknowledged the courtesy by biting scarcely hard enough to break the bone.

"In retrospect," Uncle Jack observed, "it seems odd that no one had given any thought at all as to what might be used for a ball and bat." A parley was held, and the Oklahoma pitcher who had brought the nine-pound cannon balls from

The Battle of the Wilderness was hurt and disgusted that he would not be allowed to hurl them at the Kansas batters. As a balm to his damaged pride, the Kansas team graciously voted to allow him to pitch porcupines, if he could find any, every other inning.

While this was going on, one of the Oklahomans had ripped a post from Uncle Jack's fence, and all agreed it would make an elegant bat. As to the ball: one of the local Kansas boys announced that he had a sort-of real baseball at home, and he was dispatched on the fastest pony to fetch it.

In the meantime, rather than delay the game any longer, Uncle Jack went to the root cellar and selected a fine baseball-sized potato.

Aunt Tildy admonished him to be careful with it because it was *supper*. Uncle Jack tried to put her mind to rest by saying, "The Oklahoman has yet to be born who can hit any potato I pitch. And when suppertime arrives, I shall eat this one with special relish."

Aunt Tildy, who tended to take things literally, started to tell him that they had no relish, special or otherwise, but Uncle Jack was already loping toward the pitcher's mound.

5

The Game

Uncle Jack admitted that the debacle which followed was due solely to his lack of experience in hurling potatoes at Oklahomans. "Given a few weeks," he said, "a good supply of potatoes and a few Oklahomans to throw at, I know I could have done better."

"I am convinced I put everything I had into that pitch," Uncle Jack said. "When that potato left my hand, it flew like a cannon ball in The Battle of the Wilderness."

The Oklahoma batter had taken a few practice swings with the fence post and seemed to be pleased with it. "By golly," Uncle Jack said, "he held it like he loved it! I expect the bark on that fence post probably reminded him of the skin on girls in Oklahoma.

"Well, the long and the short of it is, I know in my heart that potato suffered no pain. As we learn from Genesis, 3:19, 'Dust thou art, and unto dust shalt thou return.' In all my years in Kansas, I have never seen anything more likely to be proclaimed dust than that potato when it encountered that fence post."

The Kansas infielders and the Kansas outfielders and the Kansas shortstop were left with nothing to catch, grab, or snag. The Oklahoma batter trotted in an insolent manner from base to base, then paused and bit the head off the third base rattlesnake.

Between third base and home plate, a few of the local girls under the age of nine fired their small-bore rifles at his legs, but did not even scratch him. Uncle Jack said there were no hoots or catcalls. No one blamed the girls. "Hell, it was the first ballgame for most of them. Kids got to learn."

Old One-Eyed Charlie Ebbets declared the Oklahoman "home safe."

The Kansas team called for time out to find another rattlesnake for third base. With an impartiality which was respected by all, One-eyed Charlie Ebbets flat out explained to the Oklahomans that if they didn't stop biting the heads off the third basemen, the Kansas team would not be able to establish a quorum, and Oklahoma would forfeit the game.

By agreement, each team sent one man to bat per inning. After a hit or strike-out, the field would change, and a batter from the other team would step up. If the first batter was still on a base, and the next batter hit the ball—or potato, the second runner could chase the first runner and pummel, maim or kill him. Uncle Jack claimed this arrangement made for a very fast game.

Cleatus Alworth was the first batter for the Kansas team. Uncle Jack always shook his head sadly when he talked about Cleatus. "He was just not cut out to be a ball player. His God-given talent was cracking walnuts with his teeth, and had Abner Doubleday, who invented the game, promulgated the rules of baseball along such lines as to give a person the option of swinging a bat at a ball or cracking walnuts with his teeth, the Kansas team would have shown brightly that day."

The Oklahoma pitcher viewed Cleatus with disdain and contempt, and would have blasted him off the plate except for the fact that he had nothing with which to blast. The pitcher had been unable to find a porcupine, and Aunt Tildy was standing guard at the door of the root cellar with her soap paddle ready to pound the pancreas off anyone trying for another potato.

Finally, loud *whoops* and red dust announced the return of the boy with his sort-of real baseball. The Oklahoma pitcher took the ball and thanked the lad so graciously that Uncle Jack had to revise his opinion and admit that some Oklahomans might have human blood in them.

Now, Uncle Jack claimed that what followed was probably some kind of cosmic balancing act. The pitcher was the Oklahoman with the eye inclined toward Macon, Georgia (the same soap-eating scalawag who had offered Uncle Jack 13 ponies for Aunt Tildy). Poor old Cleatus had lost the sight of his left eye due to damage to his optic nerve from cracking walnuts with his teeth.

The pitch went in low and fast, and the Oklahoma catcher had nabbed it and stood picking his teeth by the time Cleatus swung the bat, which Uncle Jack estimated to be between three and four minutes later. One-Eyed Charlie

Ebbets called, "Strike one."

Uncle Jack was never one to speak ill of a neighbor. He said what happened next was just over-compensation, pure and simple. To redeem himself for looking like a fool the first time, Cleatus swung the bat before the next ball was even pitched. Uncle Jack said anyone might have made the same mistake, although in fairness to mankind at large, he admitted to having known few to make such a damn stupid mistake.

In fairness, Cleatus was admired for putting everything he had on that swing. Unfortunately, the momentum whirled Cleatus around in such a manner that the fence post burst the catcher's head like a ripe pumpkin. He was dead before he hit the ground.

To his credit, Old One-eyed Charlie Ebbets immediately declared it a foul and, possibly, a misdemeanor, and penalized Cleatus five yards. When Uncle Jack pointed out that a five yard penalty would put the batter behind the catcher, Charlie said, "Well, damnation! Then, if he makes a hit on the next pitch, he must hop to first base on one leg."

Uncle Jack said Charlie Ebbets was as fair as any man who ever lived.

Cleatus didn't hit the next pitch. And he didn't kill anyone else either because the new catcher was standing back near the Barber County line.

What with the delay while the Kansas team was being organized, and the delay while finding a ball and bat, the sun was starting on its downward slide. One promising Kansas player had died of a bitten-off head, and one Oklahoma player had died from standing too close to Cleatus Alworth. The score was one to naught in favor of Oklahoma, and Oklahoma was again at bat.

The batter was a small but well-built man. Uncle Jack judged him to have been sired around Ardmore, with maybe about 23% Enid blood in him. Uncle Jack threw the ball so as to wipe off the batter's chin, but his confidence was still shaken from the potato debacle, so it only tore off part of his ear. This seemed to annoy the fellow, and his bat sucked up red dust as he took a couple practice swings.

With his next pitch, Uncle Jack felt the sadness of knowing that his pitching days were over. The Oklahoma batter happened to be the one who owned the red sock and was letting it dangle out of his shirt pocket in an insulting and taunting manner. He connected, and there was no way he could fail to run the bases and reach home plate.

Well, there was one obstacle. As the runner passed third and sprinted for home, one of those sweet little girls raised her .22 rifle in the best spirit of sportsmanship and fired below the knee.

But the shot went high, and the Oklahoman fell dead nine feet from home plate. It probably should have been called a foul, but the girl was so upset that she won the sympathy of all, including old Charlie Ebbets.

Uncle Jack said he had always felt badly about that episode because anybody can make a mistake. The poor thing declared she "just hated baseball" and would never play it again. Uncle Jack worried that the future of baseball in the United States of America looked very bleak if fathers did not spend more time teaching their children how to use firearms,

At the bottom half of the second inning, Uncle Jack stepped in and picked up the fence post-bat. He sensed an ugly feeling emanating from the Oklahomans. He described it as "almost a hostility."

That puzzled Uncle Jack, "Because," he said, "even with two of them dead and one in serious condition from having inadvertently stepped on the first base Kansas rattlesnake during the rifle fire, they still had the numerical advantage."

The score was still Oklahoma one, Kansas naught. After the first pitch, old One-Eyed Charlie Ebbets cried, "STRIKE!" With the second pitch, Uncle Jack swung and felt the sting of contact all through his hands and arms.

"That ball was headed, without benefit of passport or immigration papers, all the way into Arkansas," he said.

Uncle Jack pranced proudly, perhaps arrogantly, around the bases, encouraged by the gleeful rattling of the off-duty first and third basemen. When he was about twelve feet from home plate the Oklahoma pitcher bowled one of the nine-pound cannon balls, which he had placed near the pitcher's mound, and struck Uncle Jack in the ankle. The game was over.

It was not over because one Kansas player had been injured. It was over because Aunt Tildy saw Uncle Jack writhing on the ground in pain and rushed to the pantry, filling her apron pockets with three-day-old Godamighty cocklebur biscuits. It was over because, on the way to the batter's area, she swooped up her soap paddle. Assuming the batter's stance, Aunt Tildy, tossed a Godamighty cocklebur biscuit into the air and smacked it viciously with the soap paddle. Again and again and again—like a Gatling gun—those stickley biscuits covered with globules of lye soap cut through and laid waste to the Oklahoma horde.

"It was like grape-shot at The Battle of the Wilderness," Uncle Jack shouted.

The Oklahomans fled—although Uncle Jack would

have called "fled" a weak and inadequate word—leaving their dead and wounded where they lay.

The sun sank on Comanche County. It was doubtlessly damn glad to do it. Maybe it saw Uncle Jack rocking back and forth rubbing his painful ankle. Maybe it heard Uncle Jack shouting in the general direction of Oklahoma, "*Ad Astra Per Aspera*, you rotten scalawags! *Ad Astra Per* goldang *Aspera!* Just read your Bible!"

6

The Trend of History

My first year of College was a time of sad awakening for me. The department of history at the university would not acknowledge the importance of the Kansas-Oklahoma baseball game or the bowling of a Battle of the Wilderness cannon ball against Uncle Jack's ankle.

"This is not the trend of Kansas history today," I was told.

Any historian who wants to be taken seriously today must find the diary of some...say...nine-year-old girl who came to Kansas in a covered wagon and was kidnapped by a left-handed renegade—a renegade who lived in comfort with the Indians as his friends, because ever since he arrived, the buffalo had been plentiful. "If at all possible," my professor said, "it would help if the girl were double-jointed and deaf."

It profited me nothing to point out that, North, South, East and West, library shelves were sagging with such books. "How about," I suggested in disgust, "a book wherein a girl gets captured by Indians and accidentally bites her lip and develops a nasty canker sore?"

"That's about the silliest thing I ever heard," the professor replied. "…But, wait! Maybe if she had a club-foot…!"

Discouraged, I trudged back to my chilled room at the boarding house thinking I had forgotten to mention to the professor some crucial detail Uncle Jack or Aunt Tildy had told me.

7

Uncle Jack and the G.A.R.

Two months after the ball game, Uncle Jack was still favoring his left ankle and had started referring to himself as the last casualty of the Civil War. He sat, with swollen, elevated ankle on the small front porch; sat unable to harvest the meager crops or prepare the fields for the next meager crops; sat unable to properly tend his cattle. Fortunately, there was enough rain that year, and their few cattle found enough grass to survive on. Able only to watch the rattlesnakes and cockleburs copulate, he found the contentment which comes with understanding. "I began to understand," he told me, "the probable origin of Oklahomans."

Years later, Aunt Tildy told me the incapacitation from that ankle wound gave Uncle Jack too much time to think. She said a mind like Uncle Jack's should be kept busy straightening bent nails or picking the meat out of walnuts. It worried Uncle Jack's mind how he would provide a living if he could no longer farm or run the ranch. He pondered the possibilities of braiding rattlesnakes in pleasing and decorative ways so as to create a new fashion for the ladies back East, but Aunt Tildy told him she had neither the time nor the inclination to gather the raw materials for such an endeavor. When he proposed making curry combs from cockleburs, Aunt Tildy chose not to hear.

Being the last person wounded in the Civil War began to take on a serious significance to Uncle Jack. He knew veterans such as his neighbor, Oliver Hoskins, received pensions from the government. Uncle Jack was willing to wager that none of their ankles hurt any worse then his own.

With the cannon ball from the Battle of the Wilderness in front of him on the kitchen table as a glaring reminder of his pain and suffering, Uncle Jack applied for membership in the Grand Army of the Republic.

Now, the G.A.R. was an organization of veterans who had fought for the Union. A fraternal organization in the beginning, they became a strong force in American politics. Besides helping their members obtain pensions, Aunt Tildy said, they wore fine uniforms, and some of them got to carry swords. Aunt Tildy figured Uncle Jack coveted wearing a uniform and carrying a sword as much as he coveted a pension. Upstairs, years later, we opened the trunk containing

Uncle Jack's correspondence. This is what we found:

Oct. 4, 1902

Mr. Josiah Pemburton
Post Commander, G.A.R.

Dear Sir,

It is my honor and pleasure to take pen in hand and apply for membership in your Organization. Due to lack of foresight and, perhaps, some reticence on the part of my parents, I was not born until 1865, the year the hostilities ended. Otherwise, I would have been there with you every inch of the way.

Nevertheless, in August last, I was wounded in the ankle by a slow-moving cannon ball from the Battle of the Wilderness. It hurt like hell, making me probably the last casualty of the Civil War.

I understand some of you fellows are drawing a pension from the Government, and I feel it would behoove me to do likewise. Also, how much does the uniform and sword cost?

Please be assured that in parades I can limp as well as the worst of the others. This really does hurt like hell.

Yrs. Truly,
Jack Freeman

Stored with this draft was its response from the G.A.R. Post Commander:

Oct.10, 1902

Mr. Jack Freeman

Dear Sir,

In regard to your application for membership in the Grand Army of the Republic, and
in regard to your claim to be the last casualty
of the Civil War, and in regard to your claim
to have been hit by a cannon ball from the
Battle of the Wilderness—we have serious
reservations.

In the first place, according to your appli-
cation, you were not born until 1865. The
Battle of the Wilderness was fought in 1864.
You state that you received your wound in
August, 1902.

$$\begin{array}{r} 1902 \\ -1864 \\ \hline = 38 \text{ years} \end{array}$$

In the second place, our Sergeant-at-
Arms, who was a corporal of artillery during
the previously aforementioned war, assures
us that though the Confederate artillery was
slow, often to the point of being boring, it
was never known to be *thirty-eight*
years late.

In the third place, your application is
denied!

Respectfully Yrs.

Josiah Pemburton

Uncle Jack did not hesitate to respond. A draft of his
second letter was included:

Oct. 19, 1902

Josiah Pemburton
Post Commander, G.A.R.

Dear Sir,

I take umbrage at your indication that I
am not entitled to the benefits provided for
those of us who suffered grievous wounds
from The Battle of the Wilderness. Like most
everything else bad which happens, the long
delay in being hit by a cannon ball from the
Battle of the Wilderness was caused by the
damned Oklahomans, who thought I was
sending a smoke signal inviting them to a
baseball game, which I was not.

In the hope that this will clear things
up...

...I remain, Yr. Obd. Svt.
Jack Freeman

There came no answer. Aunt Tildy said Uncle Jack
paced the floor, limping in a most protracted manner. He
limped with a touch of pride as one might limp had one
received an ankle wound from a cannon ball from the Battle
of the Wilderness.

But there came no answer.

When Oliver Hoskins died, he was buried in his
Masonic apron and, perhaps, other items of apparel. I'm not
sure. At any rate, I *know* he was not buried in his G.A.R.
uniform or with his G.A.R. sword because Uncle Jack
bought them from the widow for six dollars. She mentioned
that for the right price she might be able to retrieve the

Masonic apron, but Uncle Jack told her not to bother.

Oliver Hoskins had been smaller than Uncle Jack, more slender across the shoulders and shorter in the leg. But the weave and the thread were wonderfully supple; Uncle Jack and the uniform seemed, somehow, to "adapt"—one to the other.

From the eaves of his front porch Uncle Jack suspended a head-bumping sign that read, "*G.A.R. Post #1000.*"

It did not bother Uncle Jack a whit that there might be another, more genuine G.A.R. post #1000. It didn't bother him half-a-whit. When anyone questioned his right to have his own personal and exclusive G.A.R. post, Uncle Jack would say, "Here's the cannon ball—and here's my ankle."

Aunt Tildy said, "There weren't many who chose to argue with that!"

8

Jack Freeman, God's Gift to Science

Aunt Tildy remembered that, as October 1902 waned and November threatened starvation and doom, Uncle Jack persevered and dared the world from the front yard. With a Battle of the Wilderness cannon-ball-to-the-ankle-type wound, a stretched-almost-too-tight-uniform, and a lovely G.A.R. sword with an ivory hilt, he menaced, decapitating and eviscerating cockleburs. He wished for an encounter with a few rattlesnakes, but they were tucked in for the winter. "In general," Aunt Tildy said, "he was tramping out the vintage with his terrible swift sword."

The front yard is where the mailman found him. As though such sights greeted him at every stop, he simply said, "Afternoon, Jack."

Uncle Jack, who could turn a phrase as well as the next man, said, "Afternoon, Abner. Care to place your order for the spring crop of rattlesnakes?"

"Oh, no, I guess we're still pretty well fixed for rattlesnakes," he replied, handing Uncle Jack an already-opened envelope. It had been addressed to the Postmaster, but that part had been scratched over and a notation added: "Give this to Jack Freeman." It was from a kid in central Kansas:

> To whom it may concern:
>
> This letter has been passed on to you as a result of the high esteem held for you by your local postmaster. I have sent this letter to post-masters across the state requesting that they be forwarded to the most educated citizen in the County.

(Aunt Tildy told me she was pretty sure it was at this point of the letter when Uncle Jack sat heavily on the front step and uttered a word which most likely had been borne in on the wind from Oklahoma.)

> First, allow me to introduce myself. My name is George F. Sternberg. As you undoubtedly know, thousands of years ago Kansas was covered by an inland sea. It is my pursuit in life to find and study the fossil remains of sea life from that period.
>
> I am appealing to citizens such as yourself to survey your area for such fossils and report your findings to me for possible fur-

ther study.

While I have found at least fifty fine fish fossils, my most cherished desire is to find the fossil of a fish-in-the-belly-of-another-fish.

I eagerly await your correspondence.

Respectfully Yrs.

George F Sternberg

Aunt Tildy considered that letter a personal gift to her from God. It didn't bother her that she was the only woman in the world who was the wife of a whole G.A.R. post. And it was not an excessive inconvenience when the Post Commander appointed her President of the Lady Auxiliary of G.A.R. Post #1000. The potluck dinners were no trouble because that's what was for supper anyway. What began to pall, she said, was being required to stand in the hot sun batting off rattlesnakes and cockleburs while Post #1000 performed full-dress parades up and down the road.

Sometimes, when the Post was new, she said, there might be three or four parades a day. The *Grand* Post Commander (Aunt Tildy said Uncle Jack had declared it within his dominion and power to grant himself a promotion for a job well done) was usually followed in parade-order by his sons: Art, Ben and Charlie, and his daughter, Little Lucy. Art usually carried a makeshift flag. Ben usually beat on a makeshift drum, and Charlie counted cadence in what he claimed was Roman numerals. The sweet little girl, Little Lucy, who brought up the rear, sometimes carried a small dead bird which, Aunt Tildy said, made as much sense as any of the rest of it.

Aunt Tildy used to shake her head and wonder to me if

a civil war was really worth doing.

Uncle Jack's life found a new focus with the receipt of that letter from Mr. George Sternberg. In the upstairs trunk containing Uncle Jack's correspondence I found this draft of his answer to Mr. George F. Sternberg:

Oct. 26, 1902

Mr. George F. Sternberg

Dear Sir,

It was an honor to receive your letter and a genuine delight to make the acquaintance of someone who shares my life-long interest in the study of science. My personal field of endeavor is the study of *Oklahomus Erectus*. The focus of my research on this almost-unbelievable specie is to determine if *Oklahomus Erectus* is going *up* or going *down* the evolutionary ladder. I'll tell you, Mr. Darwin could have saved himself a lot of time and money and still had plenty to scratch his head about if he had gone to Oklahoma instead of the Galapagos Islands.

I, also, have had a lifelong interest in fossils and gather them whenever possible. It is difficult to believe that my ranch in Comanche County was ever part of an inland sea. More likely, an inland desert!

Even so, I have found numerous fossils in this area. It was only four days ago I was perusing the terrain with my wife, who is also my field assistant, when I discovered a wondrous fossil. I could not contain my excitement, and exclaimed, "Tildy, look what the Lord hath delivered into my hands!"

What I had found was the fossil of a cockroach with another cockroach in it's belly. At the present time this fossil is safely ensconced at the base of Tildy's cactus plant. If this fossil would be of use to you I would be happy to ship it to you, *per gratis*.

In the meantime, I shall endeavor to find you a fine fossil fish-with-another-fish-in-its-belly. I do not anticipate it will take long, so you may expect a package from me forthwith.

Yrs. In Science,
Jack Freeman

Aunt Tildy told me that upon posting this letter, Uncle Jack doffed his G.A.R. uniform and laid aside his G.A.R. sword with the ivory hilt. The cockleburs and rattlesnakes were left to their own devices, and a grievous wound from the Battle of the Wilderness was miraculously healed, or at least held in abeyance. From that moment on, Uncle Jack dedicated his life and fortune to science.

After three days of tramping over the countryside with a magnifying glass and prodding and poking every outcropping of rock, Uncle Jack began to show signs of fatigue.

"Truth to tell," he announced to Tildy, "I am a little amazed at how few fossils of fish-with-other-fish-in-their-bellies I am finding."

Aunt Tildy was experiencing the joy of living with a field-scientist, one who was gone most of the day, rather than a wounded hero or a Grand Commander of the G.A.R.

who was always underfoot. It is my speculation that Aunt Tildy understood the workings of her husband's mind better than he did. At any rate, she had spent the morning searching the pages of the Bible so that when Uncle Jack's words of defeat and discouragement left his lips, she was primed, cocked, and ready to fire:

"Hebrews, 10:36," she told him. "For ye have need of patience, that, after ye have done the will of God, ye might receive the promise."

Then she quoted Job 12:8: "Speak to the earth and it shall teach thee: and the fishes of the sea shall declare unto thee."

Whenever Aunt Tidy told me that story she always said she felt a little guilty about using Biblical abuse against Uncle Jack. She believed, what with the flying open of his mouth and the resultant falling out of his briar pipe, and the breaking of the bit off it, she had caused a "light stroke."

Undoubtedly questioning the wisdom of teaching women to read, Uncle Jack returned to the fossil fields. Oh, he made some interesting finds and, at first, he fired off letters to Master George F. Sternberg:

Nov 11, 1902

Master George F. Sternberg

Dear George,

Today I made an exciting find! I was studying the side of a small gully which had been created once when it rained in Comanche County, and I found the fossil of a crawdad-with-another-crawdad-in-its-belly! I am sure this item will be a welcome

addition to your research.
I eagerly await your reply.

Yrs. Truly,
Jack Freeman

The reply was short and undated:

Mr. Freeman,

I can understand your excitement in finding a cockroach-with-another-cockroach-in-its-belly, and I can understand your excitement in finding a crawdad-with-another-crawdad-in-its-belly. I have witnessed this excitement in amateurs many times. The prize I seek, however, and the only one I consider worthwhile, is a *fish* with another *fish* in its belly.

G.F.S.

Aunt Tildy said that letter had a severe dampening effect on Uncle Jack's enthusiasm. He sat around the house reading and rereading Mr. Sternberg's reply. The Battle of the Wilderness cannon-ball-wounded ankle seemed to grow painful once again.

The weather had turned cold, and the wind had a sharp chill in it as Uncle Jack returned to the fossil fields. Each day he became more despondent. Monday he plopped onto the kitchen table a fossilized armadillo-with-another-armadillo-in-its-belly. Tuesday it was a fossilized mud-turtle with what appeared to be a fossilized celluloid collar button in its belly. Aunt Tildy told me Uncle Jack was approaching a state of near devastation.

She asked if he planned to write Mr. George F.

Sternberg about the armadillo and the turtle, but he said, "Nope, Sternberg didn't even date his letter."

It was on a Friday, about 2:30 in the afternoon, Aunt Tildy told me, when she was nearly frightened to death by a loud *whooping* and *whooping* which seemed to be approaching the house at a great rate of speed. She rushed to open the door. "Jack seemed to be in such a state I was afraid he would just bust through it, without noticing"

"By the great, good, living God, I have found it, Tildy! 'Thou hast made me a little lower than the angels, and hast crowned me with glory and honor.' Psalms, 8:15! Son-of-a-bitch!"

Aunt Tildy said she did not know how "anyone under the light of the living sun could have carried that great chunk of limestone at all, much less carry it while loping and *whooping*."

Uncle Jack took pen in hand and wrote:

December 3, 1902

Dear Georgie!

The Good Book tells us in Hosea, 4:3: "The fishes of the sea also shall be taken away." Well, sir, I most joyously announce that I have found our fish and taken it away. It lies before me at this instant on the kitchen table! I present you with your fossilized dream, Sir: a fish-in-the-belly-of-another-fish!

At first glance, the belly-fish does not precisely accommodate our understanding of how a fish might reasonably be expected to look. This fish is completely round and about three inches in diameter. I would judge its thickness to be one and one-half inches. Though the label is, of course, completely deteriorated, there can be little doubt that this is a *can of tuna!!!*

On receipt of your telegram I shall board the soonest train and personally place this prize in your hands.

Yrs. for the glory of science and God,
Jack Freeman

Aunt Tildy said Uncle Jack allowed a few days for the letter to reach George F. Sternberg and then placed a chair at the front window. With a telescope he watched for the telegraph boy. She told me it was no inconvenience to place his meals nearby on the end-table.

It would be unfair to Uncle Jack to suggest that all his time was spent in that chair. He also paced and fretted. He cleaned and oiled his fossil-finding gear, paced and fretted—and sat in that chair.

The days dragged along with painful slowness, but Uncle Jack displayed little sign of discouragement. Then on New Year's day of 1903, he donned his G.A.R. Grand Commander's uniform and buckled on his ivory-hilted G.A.R. sword. With a few words, which conceivably might have been a prayer but most likely was an opinion concerning George F. Sternberg's lineage, he dumped the whole fossil collection into the well.

Aunt Tildy said she wished Uncle Jack had not done that because she could taste a difference in the water afterwards. She said the tuna had doubtless gone bad.

9

Sin in Comanche County

Sin, in Comanche County, was much the same in the old days, I guess, as it is now. Some eschew it, some embrace it, and most don't give it much thought, unless they are the one being sinned against.

I believe, in his younger years, Uncle Jack may well have leaned a little heavily on the embracing and tended, somewhat, to eschew the eschewing. But which of us is to judge? I am pretty sure Uncle Jack's early life was not a bed of nasturtiums and therefore he might well be forgiven a few indiscretions.

Well, one time I knew a fellow up in Sedgwick County who told me his life, far from being a bed of roses, had been more like a bed of *marigolds*. By grab, if there is anything that smells worse than a bed of marigolds I would appreciate hearing of it.

So I gave him $17 for a one-way ticket to Colorado where he could live with his half-sister and her husband, who by all accounts was a no-account scalawag. Monday through Friday he drank to excess, and on the weekends he tended to overcompensate for his weekday relative sobriety.

Now, I believe it was about eleven months after this fellow went to Colorado, I heard that he had passed on. So I wrote to the County Clerk and inquired as to the cause of his death. She wrote back and said that the death certificate was a scribbledy thing, but as near as she could tell, he had died because of *avocado*. Having time on my hands and the required postage, I reasonably inquired if *avocado*, in Colorado, was a noun or a verb. She replied in what I considered a prompt and kindly manner that there was a squiggle on the end of the word which might, just possibly, be an "ly." So, he had likely died of an adverb. I expect that death *by avocado, with adverbial complications* would be a terrible-poor way to die.

On those summer days when I walked down the streets of Coldwater with Uncle Jack, I could not but notice folks crossing the street ahead of us. Some tended to leave our side of the street when they spotted Uncle Jack approaching; these folks doubtless considered him a sinner. Others crossed to our side to shake Uncle Jack's hand and wish him well; maybe they could see both sides of him.

One lady who was so prominent I shall not divulge her name, always crossed to our side of the street because she knew Uncle Jack would find a way to unobtrusively goose her. Then she would say, "Well! I never!" and Uncle Jack would say, "Don't try to tell *me* that you *never*."

But for the most part, Uncle Jack was respected by the influential and wealthy and also by those who had nasty scars running the length of their faces and parts of their ears gnawed off.

As I said, it's not my intent to be judgmental. If his early life was anything like his later life, for instance, getting ankle-wounded by a Battle of the Wilderness cannon ball 37 years too late—it behooves one to show a little Christian forbearance.

In these times we hear a good deal about the importance of a child having a role model. It is one of the blessings of my life that I have never been called upon to be one—a role model, that is. It is likely also a blessing to the children.

It's not as if I have noticed a multitude of young folks struggling to be first in line for my advice, but if ever any do, I will tell them this: Choose a mediocre role model.

Now, here are the reasons for this advice. If you set your sights and adjust your windage in the general direction of sainthood, and then choose a role model who is far and beyond your ability to equal, you will become discouraged and fall into a life of sin.

By the same token, if you have your heart set on a life of sin and take as your role model a fellow who has seven generations of son-of-a-bitchery in his blood, you will likely give the whole thing up and become a saint.

It pains me to say that Uncle Jack was mediocre in any aspect, but I believe he was a perfect mediocre role model. He was just good enough, and just ornery enough that I could feel free to experiment in either direction.

I expect I was nearly 13 when I made my first sortie into the world of sin. I had little idea which sin I ought to start with. I had saved up about three dollars, so I figured I would just sample a little of each sin until my money ran out.

So one moonlight summer night I bided my time until Uncle Jack and Aunt Tildy were asleep, then sneaked away down to the barn. Even then I knew it was proper to start a night of sin with a good belt of whiskey. Uncle Jack kept a jug in the stable, so I gave it a try. When it appeared to me that I was feeling better than I had ever before felt in my life, I saddled Old Dobbin and headed off towards Coldwater to visit a house of ill-repute.

I try to impress on young people today, when I can get them to listen (which I mostly cannot), they need Education! *Education!*

"Familiarize yourself with the vocabulary of that on which you are about to embark," I tell them, "before you drink whiskey and ride off to Coldwater."

Because, see, I had no idea what went on in a house of ill-repute. But I knew it was sin, and that's what I was after—about three dollar's worth.

The door was opened by a rouged-up woman. I wasn't expecting any Sunday School teacher, but I guess I will never forget the look she gave me. She seemed to have an unpleasant demeanor for someone trying to run a successful business.

"Well, what the hell do *you* want?" she asked me.

What did I want? How would I *know* what I wanted? What could I tell her? "Please, Ma'am, three dollars worth of sin?" Or maybe I could say, "How much for a half pint of *Ill Repute*?"

I stood there catching glimpses of ladies in what I believe is called *dishabille.* Now, whatever my feelings were concerning her attitude toward potential customers, I must give the lady this: she did have a way with words. Before she slammed the door in my nearly-13-year-old face, she explained in a manner easily understood, just exactly where I should go, how I might spend profitable time with parts of my body, and, Lord, *so* many other pieces of advice! I believe that she was really good at heart. I probably just got there at a bad time.

At any rate, I rode Old Dobbin back home feeling pretty much a failure at sin. Maybe Uncle Jack *had* just been too overpowering a role model for me.

As I rubbed down Old Dobbin, I tried another slug of whiskey.

As I walked back to the house, I determined that I had been too ambitious. Maybe my next foray into sin should be goosing the first lady I met on the streets of Coldwater. If it cost me my whole three dollars, so be it. Nobody ever told me it was cheap to sin in Comanche County.

10

Fried Snow and Icicle Biscuits

In all the years it was my pleasure to know my Great Uncle Jack, a tough old hombre who sometimes carried a revolver and sometimes used it, he never treated me with anything less than kindness and respect. Although sometimes, when I turned my head quickly and found him watching me closely, I was sure he believed that there was Oklahoma blood coursing through my veins (from my mother's side).

He gave me that look on the day I said, "Uncle Jack, in those days when times were so hard, when nothing could grow except cockleburs and rattlesnakes, how in the world did you keep from starving?"

"The summers weren't bad," he finally answered, "but in the winter we lived mostly on fried snow."

Maybe I looked a little skeptical because he quickly added, "The secret to good fried snow is having your skillet good and hot before you harvest your snow. You heat the bacon grease until it almost smokes, then you roll the snow in a little flour and plop it into the hot grease. It sizzles a lot at first, but you keep rolling it around until the outside is seared. That seals the juices in, and it's mighty tasty. 'Course, that leaves no pan drippings, so you can't make gravy."

Uncle Jack sat, plainly with more on his mind. "Only one person, my grandma, could make snow gravy." Uncle Jack finally said. "Snow gravy, and icicle biscuits. *Oh!*"

He unsheathed his knife and honed it carefully on the upper part, the rougher, higher-than-a-snake-can-usually-bite part of his boot. He seemed to thoughtful himself nearly into apoplexy, then declared, "Son, you are likely too young for this, but I will plant the seed. Girls, after a certain age, grow bumps on their bodies. These are called breasts. For some reason, which I disremember, these bumps appeal to young men. Also, they (the girls) have legs which please, and, about mid-way from head to foot, a roundness, a fullness, on the part which follows the preceding part of the girl, which also often pleases and excites young men. Do you understand what I am trying to tell you?" Uncle Jack asked.

"Tits and butt," I responded. Sweet goodness gracious, by then I was nearly fourteen years of age! I had noticed!

Uncle Jack cleared his throat a few times to gain thinking space, then declared, "Be not *distracted* by these physical distractions! In your search for a wife look for one who can make fried-snow and icicle biscuits."

I will insert here that during my senior year at the University, I began a promising paper entitled "Concerning the Early Use of Fried Snow and Icicle Biscuits in Comanche County, Kansas and the Nutritional Value Thereof."

I approached the building which housed the Home Economics department with the happy heart of a scholar. Before I submitted *this* paper, I intended to have all the facts and all the figures on fried snow and icicle biscuits which had been accumulated since the beginning of time.

I soon found myself in a large classroom filled with kitchen ranges and—I especially remember—a long line of white, porcelain sinks. Well, sir, before I had reached the third white, porcelain sink, I was confronted by a large woman who I now believe was doing research on fried snow and icicle biscuits herself.

I introduced myself, but had barely started to explain my mission when, with an abruptness which can only be understood by someone who has encountered a large woman intent on hogging all the academic glory inherent in fried snow and icicle biscuits for herself, I was shown the door. In truth, I was not really *shown* the door. I only caught a brief glimpse of it as I flew through it.

Entrenched academicians are a tough lot.

Anyway, to get back to Uncle Jack, he sat a-pondering. "To be honest, I was never worth much as a farmer. I always managed to raise a little beef, though. Tildy would put the beef in jars and pour grease over the top for a seal. No, we never starved."

Uncle Jack allowed a long uncomfortable pause as he considered my worthiness. "There's another thing," he finally said. "We always had plenty of root vegetables. See, your Aunt Tildy has witch blood in her. I figure she's about 1/16 part witch. I figure it that way because, in my research, I've found that a woman with 1/32 part witch blood can grow lesser plants and flowers—especially Larkspur. A woman like Tildy, with 1/16 part witch blood, can grow root vegetables. She can grow them anytime and anywhere, regardless of the weather. No, we never starved.

"Unfortunately, your Aunt Tildy's 1/16 witch blood line seems to have a predilection for turnips. She might, for instance, plant carrots and harvest turnips. She might plant potatoes and harvest turnips." He shuddered visibly. "I have eaten enough turnips to last me through eternity."

Uncle Jack scratched a kitchen match and held it threateningly above his pipe, but his mind was elsewhere. He looked around to see if Aunt Tildy was close by, then told me in a quiet voice, "Son, if you ever marry a woman with witch blood, make sure she has at least a 1/8 part. They can grow *corn*!"

11

G.A.R. Post #1000 Gets a Bugle

Aunt Tildy said Uncle Jack was as fine a man as ever lived. He was a good husband and a good father. But he had just had too many defeats; he seemed a little subdued. His excursion into the world of fossil science had come to naught. The local G.A.R. Post had been close to *insulting* in manor when they denied his application for membership. And the G.A.R. national headquarters was threatening legal action if he did not cease and desist from pretending to be a G.A.R. Post.

This blow was softened somewhat by a clerk who enclosed a personal letter with the G.A.R. threat:

Mr. Jack Freeman,

I should not be writing this, which might seem in counteraction to the aforementioned policy of the National Headquarters of the G.A.R., for which I might be fired. So please do not mention it, because I need the job.

Your plight has touched my heartstrings because my father got his head blown off at the Battle of the Wilderness, which left him unfit to migrate to Kansas, which had been his plan.

In the packet my mother received from my father's captain was a perfectly good shoe (the right one), because it was his head which was blown off, not his foot. The package also contained his bugle.

Due to dire circumstances, we have been reduced to eating biscuits made from cockleburs and, therefore, have no further use for this bugle.

It occurs to me that, if your G.A.R. Post (however illegal it probably is) does not have a bugle, then this would be a very good bugle for your Post to have—what with your grievous connection with the Battle of the Wilderness.

I will sell you the bugle for $3.00. I can also sell you an official G.A.R. flag for $5.00, if you promise to never tell where it came from. I can also sell you a photograph of the Ladies Auxiliary of a G.A.R. Post from the Boston area for 50¢, but cannot, in good

faith, recommend this latter item because
they are a pretty unpleasant-looking lot. If
you can use the shoe, you can have it for 35¢,
plus postage.

Hoping to hear from you soon!

Sincerely,
Henry Spicklemeir

Uncle Jack answered:

Mr. Henry Spicklemeir

Dear Sir,

Received your welcome letter concerning the Battle of the Wilderness bugle. I
am saddened to learn of your father's loss of
his head and left shoe at the Battle of
the Wilderness.

I regret that the treasury of G.A.R. Post
#1000 is about $7.00 shy of having $3.00, but
I will trade you six chickens for the bugle.
(They may taste a little like turnips because
my wife is 1/16 part witch.)

I am also interested in the G.A.R. flag, but
this will have to wait until the Post's financial
condition improves.

Although I was grievously wounded in the
left ankle by a cannon ball from the Battle of
the Wilderness, my foot was not completely
severed, and I had the good fortune to retain
both my shoes.

Yr. Obdt. Svt.
Jack Freeman

A few days later Uncle Jack received this reply:

> Mr. Jack Freeman,
>
> Dear Sir,
>
> I accept your offer of six chickens in trade for my father's Battle of the Wilderness bugle. Please send them as quick as possible, and I will send the bugle with the same consideration.
>
> Sincerely,
> Henry Spicklemeir

Aunt Tildy said Uncle Jack promptly crated up the chickens upon receipt of Mr. Spicklemeir's letter and shipped them off. A couple of weeks passed and Abner, the postal rural delivery man, handed Uncle Jack a package. It might have contained the Ark of the Covenant for the reverence with which Uncle Jack accepted it.

In honor of the bugle, Uncle Jack used his Grand Commander's voice to shout, "Post #1000—Parade Order! Fall in!" If the Grand Post Commander's voice quavered, nobody mentioned it. A ragged honor guard resignedly formed itself in a ragged line to accompany the relic into its new home.

If Abner found this stop any more appalling than his other stops in Comanche County, he did not show it by word nor deed. Delaying his rounds only long enough to observe the solemn and dignified procession as it passed beneath the head-bumping "Post #1000" sign as they stepped onto the porch, Abner clicked to his horse and drove away.

Aunt Tildy told me Uncle Jack showed great patience when the bugle arrived. He laid the package gently on the kitchen table as if it might need to cool and went to don his G.A.R. uniform and his G.A.R. ivory-hilted sword. She said he was a sight to behold in that outfit: "Pure, unencumbered, solemn dignity."

He unwrapped the bugle reverently and held it aloft. "Behold the *shofar*, the sacred ram's horn of the synagogue!"

Aunt Tildy said it didn't look that sacred to her. She said she could not doubt it had been through the Battle of the Wilderness—that, *and* First and Second Manassas, Gettysburg, Chickamauga and every other battle which was fought before Mr. Spicklemeir's father's head was blown off and his left shoe misplaced.

I asked Aunt Tildy if she felt Uncle Jack had been taken on that deal.

"Yes and no," she told me. "Six of anything would have been too much payment for that poor bugle. On the other hand, I have never been too fond of chicken because it always seems to taste like turnips."

Anyway, while the Grand Commander of G.A.R. Post #1000 was experiencing a sort of religious ecstasy at the mere touch of the Battle of the Wilderness bugle, the entire Lady Auxiliary of G.A.R. Post #1000 was experiencing a sort of "I see it but I don't believe it" feeling. The rank and file members just wanted to blow on the damn thing.

Uncle Jack soon proclaimed, "This is an historic relic of national significance. It can only be played by one who has honorably served his country while at war or has suffered a grievous, though no less honorable, wound while not."

He brought the bugle to his lips in full confidence that from it such music would issue as to rival Joshua's at Jericho. At the first blast, Jericho occurred to Aunt Tildy, too. "I truly believe the walls did show some threat of tumbling down," she said.

For pure, dogged persistence in trying to memorialize and honor the Battle of the Wilderness through the medium of music, I guess not many could measure up to Uncle Jack.

Aunt Tildy, who almost always spoke of Uncle Jack with gentleness and respect, said, "He tried to learn that thing. He really tried. But as a mother, I had to consider my children's possible hearing loss and the possible loss of the walls to my house. I finally suggested that while it was a wonderful thing to make a joyful noise unto the Lord, the Lord could hear it better if the joyful noise were made outside.

"Howsome-ever, and be that as it may," she continued, "if the Battle of the Wilderness sounded anything like your Uncle Jack's bugle playing, then Mr. Henry Spicklemeir could take it as a blessing that his father's head got blown off." She did not try to explain the left shoe.

Aunt Tildy never missed an opportunity to instruct me in the way life works. "Your Uncle Jack's bugle practice, though mostly bad, was not completely bad," she said. "For certain, within a week most of the cockleburs had turned brown and died. And you couldn't find a rattlesnake with a magnifying glass. My personal opinion is that the rattlesnakes, though goodness knows they had every opportunity, had not developed an abiding interest in the Battle of the Wilderness. Your Uncle Jack had allowed them to observe the parades of the G.A.R. Post from the sidelines, but had never allowed them to actually participate in the parade. You can't really blame the rattlesnakes," she told me.

Uncle Jack did not stop trying to play the Battle of the Wilderness bugle because of boredom or lack of devotion.

Nor did he consider himself in any way inadequate because he never coaxed a sound from it which was more pleasing than that of a duck caught in the downward motivation of a cider press.

Aunt Tildy told me that one morning she found him on the front porch with the bugle cradled like a baby in his arms. "I am at fault!" he announced. "I am grievously and ashamedly at fault. This tired old hero has obviously given its life's essence in the service of its country. I shall allot it a place of honor and ask no more of it."

The magnanimity which Uncle Jack so open-heartedly bestowed in the direction of the Battle of the Wilderness bugle did not extend to the rattlesnakes. "Deserters!" he labeled them. Aunt Tildy told me Uncle Jack likely suspected that the squawk of that bugle had driven them away. But it didn't matter. Uncle Jack never completely forgave them. And when anyone would listen, Uncle Jack would explain that rattlesnakes and Oklahomans fell from the same tree.

When Aunt Tildy talked to me about this particular time in their lives, I could imagine a rattlesnake saying to his wife, "Florence, one of the reasons we came to Kansas was the promise made by the state motto, *Ad Astra Per Aspera* (To the Stars Through Difficulties.) Now, while I eagerly anticipate the *Ad Astra,* when he plays that horn, the *Per Aspera* can be a downright bitch!"

12

Uncle Jack Meets a Minion of the Emperor of China

In Uncle Jack's trunk I found a draft of his letter to Congress petitioning for a pension (rightly due to a fellow who was grievously wounded as a result of a slow-moving cannon ball from the Battle of the Wilderness). He went to his grave with the belief that he would have received a pension and had a comfortable life had it not been for "that gol-dang Chinaman." Uncle Jack sometimes told me that Oklahomans, rattlesnakes and Chinamen fell from the same tree.

It was late in his life when Uncle Jack told me about Mr. Lee, and he was no longer sure of the date. "It must have been about 1903 or 1904." he said. "Maybe 1911."

"Anyway, this here fellow appeared in Comanche County and he was a sight to behold! He came dressed in a sort of robe which was all green and silky and embroidered with dragons. His hair was black and done in a pigtail. I guess you could observe a whole train-load of Chinamen and never find a one who was half so elegant.

"When he stepped up to the hotel desk and requested a suite, the clerk told him pretty bluntly that they did not accommodate Chinamen. Well, sir, this good old boy poured out onto the desk a poke of gold nuggets which could have paid for paving all the roads in Comanche County and endowed an orphan's home and a pickle factory as an after-thought.

About this time the hotel owner, old Leviticus Jones, sensing trouble and disruption, waddled and blustered his way over.

"Now of course I have no way of knowing what was going on in the mind of Leviticus Jones," Uncle Jack told me. "But with my own ears, while waiting to have them exposed to the light of day in the barber shop, I have heard Leviticus Jones declare that when he made his fortune, he intended to sail to the Sandwich Islands and marry a nubile princess with massive thighs and some name like 'Koonywannahoony.'

"'Excuse me, Sir.' Leviticus told that China fellow, 'I am the owner of this establishment, and I could not help but overhear the unpleasantness which has just transpired. What this fool meant to say was that we prefer not to accommodate anyone *but* gentlemen of the Chinese persuasion.'

"That Chinaman pulled out another poke of gold, and Leviticus Jones said, 'Senior, you have just bought yourself the finest hotel east of a mile west of here.'"

Uncle Jack told me that old Leviticus Jones just scooped up that gold and sort of evaporated. Uncle Jack was convinced that old Leviticus caught the first boat to the Sandwich Islands and Koonywannahoony and set about to raise a tribe of little club-sandwiches and canopies. (I never could tell when Uncle Jack was serious or when he was just checking me for traces of Oklahoma blood.)

In the days that followed, this Chinese gentleman, Mr. Lee, established himself as the sole representative of the Emperor of China in Comanche County. He bought a four-wheel buggy with yellow wheels and a team of high-stepping horses and went around and about the county explaining at each farm that the Emperor had decided to build a railroad from China to Butterfly, Kansas.

Of course, until Mr. Lee bought the hotel, there had been no Butterfly, Kansas. The town itself was called "Sourgut." Regrettably, the reason for this name has been covered by the sands of time.

But, since the Emperor of China desired it, and since "Butterfly" better reflected and projected the growing cultural awareness of the citizens of modern Comanche County, the town became, "Butterfly."

According to Mr. Lee, every morning when the Emperor of China woke and realized there was not a town named Butterfly in the county of Comanche in the state of Kansas, his heart wept. The Emperor was inordinately fond of butterflies.

So one day the Emperor of China had called Mr. Lee to the Imperial Throne Room and said, "Dammit, Mr. Lee, just lookit! We've got rice out the ying-yang, but rattlesnakes and cockleburs have we none. My people have an insatiable and unrequited need and desire for these items! Hie you off and build a railroad from China to Butterfly, Kansas. Going out, the trains will carry rice to Comanche County. Coming back, the trains will bring rattlesnakes and cockleburs to China. I don't know why I never thought of it before!"

"But Honorable Emperor, there *is* no Butterfly, Kansas. In my humble opinion, therefore, there may be difficulties in building a railroad thereto," said Mr. Lee.

"Gol-dang it!" the Emperor replied, "Gol-dang it!"

Then he handed Mr. Lee 67 pounds of gold nuggets and ordered him to hie himself to the Golden Mountain of Kansas and do his Emperor's bidding.

That was pretty much the story Mr. Lee told the locals— that, and the fact that 67 pounds of gold nuggets did not seem to go as far as they used to.

So Mr. Lee established an office in his hotel and caused two signs to be painted and affixed thereon: "Office of the Honorable China-Butterfly R.R.," " and "Butterfly, Kansas Post Office."

Mr. Lee rented the large front room in the upstairs of the hotel to the Masonic Lodge, but when Pat O'Mallay presented himself as the Comanche County embodiment of the Knights of Columbus and requested a meeting hall, Mr. Lee observed that since Mr. O'Mallay was the only Knight of Columbus in Comanche County, he did not constitute a quorum. Mr. Lee explained that it would be against the laws of Confucius to transact such an arrangement but offered Mr. O'Mallay the use of the outside privy for 30¢ a month, or in perpetuity, for a flat fee of $3.00.

Mr. O'Mallay said that rate would be acceptable if he were allowed to erect a flagpole in front of the privy.

Mr. Lee said that would be acceptable and that Mr. O'Mallay could also conduct three holy pilgrimages a month to the privy, if he were so inclined.

Mr. O'Mallay said he just might be so inclined, and for a signed receipt, he paid Mr. Lee $3.00.

Uncle Jack said Mr. Lee was the slickest and smartest hombre he had ever witnessed. He said if Mr. Lee had tried to get a Congressional pension for a cannon-ball-wounded ankle, he would probably have received twelve of them by the first mail.

Anyway, Mr. Lee bought every piece of property available, which was most of it, for a pittance, and then caused this flyer to be printed and circulated:

> Citizens: The Emperor of China has impaled me to the soon need of 800 workers for the need of The Honorable China-Butterfly R.R.
>
> Experience of supreme importance is the harvesting of rattlesnakes and cockleburs. Also, please to remember Chinese proverb, "Slowly, slowly, catchee monkey!" And therefore, before The Honorable China-Butterfly R.R. can hire 800 citizens, it is unfortunate to also and therefore, have appropriate warehouses, rattlesnake-holding pens and cocklebur bins erected adjacent and for sure.
>
> You are recommended to purchase property for these business adventures adjacent to where the railroad tracks will be built, which will be in several circles, loops and diadems in the city of Butterfly, giving all the opportunity for prosperity.
>
> A recent cable from the Emperor performs

me that upon completion of this railroad, he will ship thirteen boxcars of gold nuggets and will also and, therefore, require a large and secure storage vault for the storage of thirteen boxcars of gold nuggets. The property upon which reasonable and understandably such conditions must be erected, is adjacent to the railroad tracks. It may be purchased from Mr. Lee.

With Liberty and Justice for all,
Mr. Lee

Well, word got around. Not just in Comanche County, but in Barber County and Kiowa County, and, according to Uncle Jack, it seemed like it went all over the world. There were fortunes to be made in Butterfly, Kansas. One fellow came clear from Enid, Oklahoma and bought three parcels of adjacent land from Mr. Lee.

Years later, after Uncle Jack was laid to rest with an unauthorized and possibly illegal G.A.R. medal tucked in his vest pocket, Aunt Tildy added to the story. "Your Uncle Jack," she told me, "was not a fool like most of them people. But with a much-needed official flag for G.A.R. Post #1000 being offered for $5.00, he saw the reasonableness of finding storage room for thirteen boxcar loads of gold nuggets."

So Uncle Jack designated the chicken coop "The Comanche County Gold Nugget and Chicken Facility" and started nailing flattened tin cans all over the outside of it to make it impenetrable. Aunt Tildy said it took several weeks to find enough tin cans, then flatten and nail them on. She said when he was done the chicken coop looked pretty secure. "Probably good enough for gold nuggets," she considered. "But mostly it looked like a chicken coop covered with flat tin cans."

Mr. Lee received Uncle Jack with courtesy and dignity and listened attentively to his pitch. According to Aunt Tildy, Mr. Lee seemed to be chastened and chagrined that he himself had not conceived the idea of using a tin-can-covered chicken coop as a gold nugget repository. He shook his head in admiring wonder and congratulated Uncle Jack on his wisdom and foresight.

But then he said, "Unfortunately, your land seems to be about eleven miles south of adjacent." He was clearly feeling miserable at not being able to use this valuable gold nugget storage and chicken coop when an idea hit him. "By Confucius' beard," he exclaimed, "for $200 we can build the railroad right past your ranch! The Emperor will have a safe place to store thirteen boxcars of gold nuggets, and you will become prosperous and serene from the rent." He gave Uncle Jack a long, seductive wink and added, "Even the most well-made gold nugget storage chicken coops spring leaks sometimes."

When Uncle Jack entered Mr. Lee's office, he was more in the frame of mind to be carrying away $200 than to be owing $200. But when Mr. Lee bowed Uncle Jack out the door, and then bowed again when Uncle Jack looked back, Uncle Jack was hooked. He went home and labored and belabored the following letter:

> Congress of the United States
>
> Dear Sirs and Brothers of the late War,
>   I have not previously applied to you for a
> pension because, although I was grievously

wounded in the ankle by a cannon ball from the Battle of the Wilderness, I have considered it to be my honor and patriotic duty to suffer my pain and poverty in silence. The pension I must now request need not be a thing which goes on and on forever, but just a lump sum of $200 in the form of a check made out to the Emperor of China.

I also respectfully suggest that you consider establishing a school in Oklahoma to teach Oklahomans the difference between a burning hay stack and an invitation to a baseball game.

Yr. Obd. Svt.
Jack Freeman

Uncle Jack took the letter to the Chinaman's post office in Butterfly and paid for Mr. Lee's chop mark in lieu of a U.S. postal stamp. Then he sat, rocking, on his front porch because there was no back porch. Aunt Tildy believed he was pondering how well the average Emperor of China understood the annual leakage of a gold nugget chicken coop in Comanche County.

Every week Uncle Jack appeared at the post office and inquired if there was anything there for him from the Congress of the United States. Mr. Lee would tell him no and only gently mention the fact that the sooner Uncle Jack gave the Emperor of China the $200 the sooner the gold nugget chicken coop could start leaking.

The long and the short of it turned out to be that one day Mr. Lee was gone. Just gone. And with him had gone most of the milk and honey of the land called Comanche County.

Folks who had worn the soles of their boots down to where only *The Coldwater Talisman* separated their feet from the soil, in the pursuit of serenity and prosperity, were stunned.

"Damn and crap!" they explained to one another.

Rattlesnake pens and cocklebur bins were abandoned unfinished. The three vaults under construction capable of holding thirteen boxcar loads of gold nuggets proved to be a long-lasting embarrassment. But Uncle Jack said embarrassments are always long-lasting. He said an untold number of Christians and at least one Oklahoman had been duped out of their life savings. It was just one more gol-dang *per Aspera.*

Before the angry mob of cheated citizens burned the Chinaman's hotel, they searched through everything. What they found was mostly a large pile of mail, all sporting Mr. Lee's chop mark in lieu of U.S. postal stamps. Included in the pile was Uncle Jack's pension petition to the Congress of the United States.

Aunt Tildy told me that aside from Mr. Lee, the only person who came out ahead on The Honorable China-Butterfly Railroad scheme was the Knight of Columbus, Mr. Pat O'Mallay. He appeared to have a strong legal claim to the outside privy and the flagpole and the right to conduct pilgrimages to it three times a month or into perpetuity, which ever came first.

She said that what with their meeting house having been burned to the ground, the Masons took umbrage with the word "perpetuity" because it sounded Latin to them; they said it sounded Romish—Popish. Aunt Tildy told me a vote was taken and the Masons voted five to zero to never have any truck with either the Emperor of China or the Pope.

I guess the word got around, because neither the Emperor nor the Pope ever showed their face in Comanche County.

It was the Wednesday after the fire when the Masons confronted Mr. Pat O'Mallay about his interpretation of his contract. "As I understand it," Mr. Pat O'Mallay replied, giving them his cold, Catholic stare, "'perpetuity,' means 'perpetuity!'"

Aunt Tildy said the Masons scratched their heads, shifted their feet, and grumbled. Finally the head Mason said, "Well, as long as you understand that that's what it means."

Aunt Tildy pondered and finally said, "I have concluded from my reading of history that history without footnotes does not carry much weight. And so here's a footnote: within a week of Mr. Lee's departure, another Chinese fellow stepped off the train in Butterfly. He was shot thirteen times before he had gone fourteen steps. Your Uncle Jack said that was just the Chinaman's *Per Aspera.*"

Uncle Jack was especially proud that almost before the Chinaman hit the ground there were nineteen offers of a burial site, and all of them were on "adjacent" ground.

"Gol-dang," Uncle Jack had said, "that just demonstrates the pure *Ad Astra* of the people of Kansas."

13

Lieutenant Jack O'Hare

With the disappearance of Mr. Lee and most of the venture capital of southern Kansas, Comanche County was a pretty glum place to be. After the second Chinaman had met his ultimate *per Aspera* and been buried adjacently, most of the citizens left Butterfly. About the only social life in Butterfly was conducted by cockleburs and rattlesnakes. They seemed, for the most part, to have prospered, and local historians will tell you that many of their descendants can be found there today.

But Uncle Jack was not to be found among the glum. He had sold a steer and was reckoned to be one of the richest men in Comanche County.

Aunt Tildy said the weight of sudden wealth did not rest easily on Uncle Jack's shoulders. He sat on the front porch and rocked and pondered. Of course, there was no question but that an official flag for G.A.R. Post #1000 would be *first* on the list of his expenditures. But, she said, it also bothered Uncle Jack that Mr. Henry Spicklemeir's father's right shoe had been separated from Mr. Henry Spicklemeir's father's Battle of the Wilderness bugle.

Then one afternoon, Uncle Jack slapped the arm of his rocking chair and said, "Gol-dang it, I cannot, in good conscience, abide the thought of Mr. Henry Spicklemeir's father's right shoe. Once, without doubt, it was a comely brogan. Must it now be left alone without succor from sandal, boot or bugle, while its mate lies amoldering reasonably adjacent to Mr. Henry Spicklemeir's father's head? These thoughts led Uncle Jack to the following letter:

Mr. Henry Spicklemeir

Dear Sir,

It is once again my pleasure to take pen in hand and renew our correspondence. Since I last wrote, the fortunes of G.A.R. Post #1000 have improved. If you can still get your hands on an official G.A.R. flag, I will buy it for $5 and assure you that I will never divulge from whence it came.

I am sure you will also be interested to learn that G.A.R. Post #1000 is about to dedicate a new museum honoring the memory of those who fought so valiantly at the Battle of the Wilderness. This museum will be housed in what was recently the Emperor of China's gold nugget storage vault. I consider it to be one of the handsomest and most secure buildings in Comanche County. Be assured, Sir, that your father's bugle will lie in a place of honor.

Now, Henry, I have been asked by the rank-and-file of Post #1000 and the Board of Directors of the Battle of the Wilderness Museum to solicit the donation of your father's right shoe for said museum. If, in your generosity, you could do this, I picture the shoe and the bugle once again united, resting forever in glory and reverence.

We eagerly await your reply.

Yr. Obdt. Svt.
Jack Freeman

Aunt Tildy said that with the wealth from the sale of the steer and the out-of-the-blue conception for the Battle of the Wilderness Museum, Uncle Jack became like his old self. She said anybody who did not want to be trampled should not have stood too near Jack Freeman.

A second letter he addressed to the Smithsonian Institution:

Dear Conferees in history and science,

As you have no doubt become aware, G.A.R. Post #1000 is in the process of creating what we expect to be the definitive museum dedicated to the Battle of the Wilderness—at least in Comanche County, Kansas.

I guess you fellows know about as well as

anybody how much money it takes to start a museum. Though it pains me to the heart to do it, I have decided to part with the extensive collection of fossils which I have spent a lifetime gathering in order to finance this project.

A few of the finer of these fossils include:

1. A cockroach with another cockroach in its belly.
2. A crawdad with another crawdad in its belly.
3. An armadillo with another armadillo in its belly.
4. A mud turtle with what appears to be a fossilized celluloid collar button in its belly.
5. A fish with a fossilized can of tuna in its belly (the label is missing).

I offer you these fine fossils at the going rate.

P.S. This sale is contingent on Tildy's willingness to let me tie a rope around her and lower her into the well.

Yr. Obdt. Svt.

Grand Commander of G.A.R. Post #1000
and Director General,
Museum of the Battle of the Wilderness,
Jack Freeman

Well, Aunt Tildy said that after due time the official G.A.R. flag arrived. Uncle Jack, in full uniform and with ivory-hilted sword, accepted it solemnly from Abner, the rural delivery man.

She said that the chicken coop *cum* Chinese Emperor's

gold nugget storage vault *cum* Battle of the Wilderness Museum had already been cleaned by the Lady Auxiliary of Post #1000 of the G.A.R. at the insistence of the Grand Commander.

The Lady Auxiliary had also been assigned the task of cutting, smoothing and varnishing a suitable pole for the flag, so there would be no undue stress placed on the Grand Commander.

At the first parade performed by Post #1000 with its new and official flag, the red dust rose up from the marchers' feet like a smoke signal. Aunt Tildy was hoping to goodness the Oklahomans didn't see it and arrive for a billiard game or a ping pong tournament.

The absence of by-standing rattlesnakes was painfully obvious to all. The Grand Commander *might* have been heard to mutter something about "perfidious Albion"; he *might* have been heard to mutter "Well, *per Aspera* on the scalawags"; but he held his head high and only slightly favored his Battle-of-the-Wilderness-wounded ankle.

Aunt Tildy told me that whenever God lays a burden on us, such as the absence of rattlesnakes at a G.A.R. parade, He often lightens that burden with a blessing.

As the marchers scruffed along through the scraggley grass and the red dust, there appeared a jack rabbit. It was a jack rabbit with a sensitive visage, a jack rabbit with a contemplative, questioning face. Its left hind foot was missing from just above the ankle, and when Uncle Jack espied that ankle-wounded jack rabbit, Aunt Tildy said there was an instant bonding and affinity. Uncle Jack brought the parade to a halt and there, on the spot, gave Mr. Rabbit a battlefield commission. "This is Lieutenant Jack O'Hare," he proclaimed. "He is a wounded hero and now an official member in good standing of Post #1000."

Aunt Tildy repeated, "When God lays a burden on you, he often lightens that burden with a blessing. Lt. Jack O'Hare *was* a blessing.

"It has been my experience, however, that about the time you start getting comfortable with your blessing, God whomps you in the back of the head with another burden. So that new burden makes the first burden seem like a piece of angle food cake. So...I just don't know. Most of the trouble in my life has been caused either by God or by the Civil War, although I never intended to offend either.

"Your Uncle Jack has always been the religious one in this family," Aunt Tildy explained. "I don't spend much time worrying about Heaven or Hell. The fact of the matter is, from what I hear I believe Purgatory would about suit me. After spending most all my life on this red-dust farm, I would prefer to stick with what I know."

I really loved Aunt Tildy. I loved the yellowy-silver of her hair. I loved the bulging veins on the backs of her tired old hands. I loved the way her gnarled old feet stood steadfastly and without questioning on the dust or mud of Comanche County.

"Your Aunt Tildy," Uncle Jack sometimes told me, "can cut through the gristle and find the gravy." I was never exactly sure what he meant by that, but it never occurred to me to question him. When Uncle Jack talked about Aunt Tildy, I never felt he was testing me for traces of Oklahoman blood.

14

More About That Damned Henry Spicklemeir

As Uncle Jack rocked and pondered, he eased his Battle-of-the-Wilderness-wounded ankle to the left. "It was just pure and simple cussed contrariness on the part of Henry Spicklemeir," he explained. "Greed," he further explained.

"When the official G.A.R. flag arrived, the package also contained a note from Henry Spicklemeir. He said his mother had passed away, so he could not donate his father's Battle of the Wilderness right shoe to the Museum. He said it would just be too much of a wrench on his soul to part with this last remaining remembrance of his father. But he also said that times were tough, and for the 35¢ mentioned in a previous letter, he would still *sell* the shoe. Uncle Jack said he guessed a wrenched soul was preferable to an empty belly.

But Aunt Tildy hinted that, in reality, Uncle Jack did not just toss off Henry Spicklemeir's note with a clever phrase.

"In reality," Aunt Tildy told me, "Jack had begun to think of this Battle of the Wilderness Museum as his Mission in Life. And he was deeply offended when Mr. Henry Spicklemeir was not willing to endure a little soul-wrenching and empty-bellyness to aid in its establishment."

"Gol-dang that hard-headed Dutchman," Uncle Jack said. "He cannot seem to understand that part of the purpose of this endeavor is to honor his own father's blown-off head and misplaced brogan!" As he wrote, his pen occasionally scratched through the writing paper:

> Mr. Henry Spiclkemeir
>
> Dear Sir,
>
> Neither I, nor the Board of Directors of the Museum of the Battle of the Wilderness feel it is our place to comment on your niggardly refusal to donate your father's right brogan to be enshrined in perpetuity at our facility.
>
> The new Aide-de-camp of Post #1000, Lt. Jack O'Hare (who also suffered grievous wounds at the Battle of the Wilderness), begs me to mention that whoever cleans up the mess when (God forbid) you pass on, will most likely just throw away that sacred relic like an old shoe.
>
> Rather than have such a thing come to pass, we have voted to offer you 23¢ for that

worn, old shoe which no one else would give
a second glance.

Yrs.

Jack Freeman, Grand Commander

I showed Aunt Tildy the draft of that letter I had found
in Uncle Jack's trunk. "Did Uncle Jack *really* appoint a
three-legged jack rabbit as Aide-de-camp of his G.A.R.
post?"

"Oh, my yes," she told me. "Yes, indeedy. They had
become the closest of friends. And had your Uncle Jack
heard you call Lt. Jack O'Hare a 'three-legged rabbit,' he
would have certainly called you on your manners. No, sir,
that rabbit was '*Lt. Jack O'Hare.*'

"I have no way of knowing what misery and what vicis-
situdes lay in the Lieutenant's early life, but I feel sure that
with the loss of his left-hind foot and ankle and somewhat
above the ankle, he had pretty much given up any hopes of
having a military career. Your Uncle Jack gave him a new
lease on life.

"Besides the battlefield commission and the appointment as Aide-de-camp of G.A.R. Post #1000, Your Uncle
Jack granted him a full pension!

"The pension did not require the help of a real G.A.R.
Post; it did not require an act of Congress. What happened
was this: Jack said, 'Tildy, give the good Lieutenant a car-
rot any time he wants one.'

"He put a pile of straw on the dirt floor in a corner of the
museum for the Lieutenant to sleep on, and above it painted little crossed flags of red, white and green because he
didn't have any blue.

"At supper I could tell he felt badly about having to use
green instead of blue, but he said he believed the loss of a

foot and ankle, and somewhat above the ankle, often brought about color-blindness, especially in rabbits.

"I figure—with such a friend and mentor as your Uncle Jack, had he ever felt compelled to offer a sacrifice, that rabbit would have been the first to hop on the altar and say, 'Take me Lord, just as I am.'"

Aunt Tildy rocked and pondered. "It never occurred to me until now, but I guess among the things I have to be thankful for in this life is that Jack never hit on the idea of offering sacrifices."

A while later, Abner, the rural postal delivery man, handed Uncle Jack a reply from Henry Spicklemeir. It was straight to the point:

Mr. Jack Freeman

35¢ or no deal!

Sincerely,
Henry Spicklemeir

Aunt Tildy told me nobody could outrage Uncle Jack like Henry Spicklemeir. Uncle Jack laid the offensive note on the floor for Lt. Jack O'Hare's perusal. Lt. O'Hare did not so much *peruse* it as he did *pee* on it. She told me that, as Uncle Jack had explained, it is not uncommon for different languages stemming from the same root to have words which are the same but have different meanings.

"I expect, in rabbit talk," he had told her, "'peruse' simply means 'to pee,' If the good Lt. O'Hare could converse with us, he would doubtlessly conjugate the verb somewhat like this: 'Today I *peruse* in the front yard. Yesterday I *perused* in the front yard. Many times I have *peruseled* in the front yard.' Some of the finest soldiers in the late war could not speak a word of English. What got *read*, and what got *peruseled* on made little difference in the end."

The wisdom, understanding and quick action demonstrated by Lt. O'Hare so pleased Uncle Jack that he predicted a captaincy for Lt. O'Hare within a month.

The terse haggling between Uncle Jack and Mr. Spicklemeir over the Battle of the Wilderness brogan went on for weeks. There were offers and counteroffers. Mr. Spicklemeir finally agreed to sell for 29¢ with the stipulation that he would remove and keep the heel. Uncle Jack counter-stipulated "Gol-dang it, the heel is the most important part!"

In the end it was Aunt Tildy who settled it. She pointed out that both Uncle Jack and Mr. Henry Spicklemeir could have each had a brand new pair of high-top boots for what they had spent on postage stamps. She gave him 35¢ of her egg money with which to buy the shoe and told him to consider it a gift from the Lady Auxiliary of Post #1000.

Uncle Jack accepted the gift with unaccustomed humility and said he would assemble an immediate parade of the Post to show his gratitude. Aunt Tildy begged off the parade, saying it would be just too embarrassing. So Uncle Jack said when times got better, he would cause a stained glass window in her honor to be installed in the west side of the Battle of the Wilderness Museum.

Once again I saw what Uncle Jack meant when he said, "Tildy can cut through the gristle and get to the gravy."

"Can you imagine?" she asked me. "A chicken coop covered with nailed-on flatted-out tin cans and a stained glass window? I couldn't sleep for weeks! It would be like a goat with a diamond in its butt."

15

Frustration

It was right at three months after he'd written, when Uncle Jack got a reply from his letter to the Smithsonian Institution. Aunt Tildy said it took him aback and caused him to question his attitudes about what was important to science. It said:

Mr. Jack Freeman
Grand Commander of G.A.R. Post #1000
And Director General of the Museum of the
Battle of the Wilderness:

Dear Mr. Freeman,

Thank you for your most interesting letter.

I have been asked to inform you that, regrettably, we have no allocated funds available for new museums.

Your offer to sell your collection of various fossils with various other fossils in their bellies caused a good deal of comment and discussion here. All felt it a shame that the label was missing from the tuna can, but research is filled with disappointments.

What we are really very eager to find, Sir, is the fossil of a *fish* with another fish in its belly. If you ever find such an item please contact us with all haste.

Yrs. etc.

"Damnation!" Uncle Jack cried upon reading the letter. "Damnation to the forth power! What is it with these people? Is there a hole in my scientific education? Did my teachers, by neglect or by purpose, exclude me from what seems to be the most important thing in the world?

"*You*, Mr. George Sternberg," Uncle Jack roared, "you want a fossil fish with another fish in its belly? You—at the Smithsonian Institution (doubtless, fossils yourselves)—*you* want fish fossils with other fish fossils in their bellies? Goldang you all! I shall go into the darkest parts of the earth and find such fossils. I shall send you both thirteen boxcar loads of fossil fish-with-other-fish-in-their-bellies, and you will be forced to build vaults in which to keep them! I shall keep sending boxcars of fossil fish long after you are dead and moldering in your graves! I shall keep sending boxcars of fossil fish unto your ninth generation! Then I shall write you each this letter: 'Dear Sir, *NOW* would you like to see a fossilized mud turtle with what appears to be a fossilized celluloid collar button in its belly? *Would one be enough? You damn well better think carefully before you answer!'"*

Uncle Jack stomped back and forth across the front porch, "sort of howling at the moon, even though it was broad daylight," as Aunt Tildy put it.

The loyal Lt. Jack O'Hare was never more than a step (or a three-legged hop) behind him. "Belligerent he was! About as belligerent and aggressive as one might ever hope a bunny rabbit to be.

"I truly believe that if the angel Gabriel or St. Paul the Apostle suddenly appeared in shining raiment and questioned your Uncle Jack's right to state his opinion concerning scientist, fish or fossil—that bunny, or more properly, Lt. Jack O'Hare, would have handed them their butts on silver platters."

Aunt Tildy could cut through the gristle and get to the gravy.

After Aunt Tildy was finally able to get enough turnip wine down Uncle Jack's throat to calm and settle him, he slept until nine o'clock the next morning.

After breakfast Uncle Jack laid the letter from the Smithsonian Institution on the floor and asked Lt. Jack O'Hare if he cared to peruse it.

"Did he peruse it?" I asked.

She said she had no idea because she had taken to bed praying God for a week-long migraine headache to relieve her life in Comanche County.

16

The Great Albanian Potato Famine

The Battle of the Wilderness brogan arrived at last, and Aunt Tildy said it was a woeful sight. It was run down at the heel, and the shoestring was partly gone and mostly rotten. The toe was warped upwardly at a painful angle, and there was an unhealthy whiteness about the tongue. But Uncle Jack was ecstatic.

Lt. Jack O'Hare, having found the bugle somewhat lacking in the social skills one hopes for in a roommate, showed the quiet hopefulness often found in three-legged bunnies who suddenly and unexpectedly find themselves breveted Lieutenant and Aide-de-camp in a G.A.R. Post. Aunt Tildy hoped that maybe the brogan could talk Rabbit

Bearing the Battle of the Wilderness brogan like a plaster image of the Holy Mother, the stately parade of G.A.R. Post #1000 proceeded past the broken cultivator and was approaching the broken plow.

In the distance, a horseless carriage belched and popped, squealed and groaned, yawed and bucked, drawing nearer, raising so much red dust that a new word might be needed to describe such a sight.

The parade, a contradiction of joy and solemnity, required little time to pass any given point. By G.A.R. standards this parade would have been no parade at all. In truth, to anyone who had ever seen a parade, this might appear to be only a family walking in single file across a small stretch of failed pasture.

The leader, the Grand Marshal, was dressed in a G.A.R. uniform which was two inches too short at the cuffs, four inches too short at the ankles, and so tight across the shoulders as to be painful, even to an observer. A fine, G.A.R. sword with an ivory hilt was suspended from his belt, and it hung at such an angle as to dangle between his ankles, causing him to trip approximately every third step. In his arms a catastrophe of a shoe hunkered down in embarrassment.

Behind the Grand Marshal a stair-step of children marched, skipped and hopped. Some waved flags; one beat on tin a pan. At least one wished she had been born into a nice family in, say, Peoria.

And last in line was a three-legged bunny rabbit, Lt. Jack O'Hare. He was doing his utmost to preserve the dignity of Post #1000 while struggling with a new prosthetic foot which had been carved that morning from a fine, straight-grained piece of cedar by Uncle Jack, the newly self-appointed Post Surgeon General of Post #1000.

Aunt Tildy said that by the time the horseless carriage arrived it was called an "automobile." She said enough of the soil of Kansas was on it and in it that the vehicle could rightly have carried its own *Ad Astra Per Aspera* flag.

The driver was a large and portly man who also carried a significant amount of the earth's soil on his person, but not enough to make a *big* state like Kansas. Aunt Tildy surmised that he was more of a "Vermont" or "Rhode Island" type.

Clearly hoping for a quick end to its misery, the automobile steamed and *chuffed* close to the path of the parade. Aunt Tildy had witnessed many deaths. She had seen some fight death with every strength they had, some welcome it, and some beg for it. She firmly believed that the car fell into the last two categories. At its passing, folks would say it a blessing—and, perhaps, remark on how natural it looked.

Aunt Tildy figured the driver, from his looks, was a preacher, a lawyer or a traveling salesman. "Or maybe," she said, "like most men, he was a little bit of each."

The fellow stood up on the floorboards of the car and clutched the steering wheel with both hands. "Madam," he said, "If I might make so bold, *what*, in the name of our Lord and Savior, is transpiring here? I was seeking the residence of Mr. Jack Freeman, but I seem to have stumbled into a loony bin."

Aunt Tildy cast a sidewise "I know, I-can't-believe-it-either" glance at the Parade Marshal, tripping over his G.A.R. sword with its ivory hilt and carrying a pitiful brogan as if it were his admission ticket to heaven. She observed the stair-step children beating tin pans and wishing they were in Peoria. And her eyes could not but linger on the game little bunny rabbit hopping along behind with the straight-grain cedar prosthesis.

"Mister," she replied, "If you have the time to explain the difference to me, I will listen with rapt attention."

If the stranger had, perhaps, through understandable amazement, gotten off to a bad start, he recovered quickly. He sized up the situation, exited his vehicle, and, although a portly man, almost *skipped* into position at the end of the parade. Aunt Tildy said he probably considered any activity before this parade to have been a deplorable waste of his life.

"White spats and a derby hat!" Aunt Tildy enthused. "He stepped in a high march-step and had not gone five feet before he broke out with 'The Battle Hymn of the Republic.' Your Uncle Jack looked back over his shoulder and nodded a dignified, ivory-hilted-sword-carrying, parade-marshal nod. He waved his G.A.R. sword over his head and pointed it at the flat-tin-can covered chicken coop G.A.R. hall.

"I guess if that poor little old shed could have taken to its heels and run for the border, it would have."

According to Aunt Tildy, Uncle Jack's dedicatory speech at the fairly secure door (it had one broken hinge) of the Battle of the Wilderness Museum was a piece of work which could be compared with the Gettysburg Address or the "Give me liberty or give me death" oratorium. She said it was a cry and a shame the speech had not been preserved for posterity, but there had been no time to take notes.

"It was the most beautiful speech I ever heard," she said.

To Uncle Jack, the arrival and parade-participation of a portly, spatted, derby-hatted man was an inspiration to beggar any previous experience he had had with inspiration.

Aunt Tildy twisted a strand of gray hair and tugged at it until bits and snatches of that day came back to her. "For a man who had never been within 700 miles and 30 years of the Battle of the Wilderness, your Uncle Jack remembered it remarkably well," she said.

If his oration leaned more heavily on the importance of bugles and right-footed brogans than on the ultimate victory of the Union army, that was understandable due to the circumstances. Uncle Jack said in battle men and horses die. They lie wounded and screaming, and it can be unpleasant. But the sight of a lost and forlorn brogan lying—well—lying lost and forlorn can bring the staunchest man to tears.

Aunt Tildy said that as she listened she could almost smell the cannon smoke and hear the case shot splattering through the leaves. She could almost hear the cries of wounded horses and men, the screech of straining leather, the clank of chains, and the rattle of drums.

The frequent references to "gol-dang Oklahomans, perfidious rattlesnakes and sons-a-bitching Chinamen" added a dimension of enrichment doubtless missed in the actual battle.

The oration ended with a prayer that while He was keeping His eye on the sparrow and the "faint and struggling seaman," He might also watch over and protect smashed bugles and forlorn right-footed brogans, which deserved so much and asked so little.

The round-bellied, white-spatted, derby-hatted stranger, who stood just behind the commissioned and pensioned and prosthezised bunny rabbit, appeared to be ecstatic. Aunt Tildy said his applause was a marvel of timing—long enough to let the speaker know he was completely appreciated and short enough not to encourage a second round.

Uncle Jack raised his arms and pronounced an *Ad Astra Per Aspera* on one and all, and the show was over.

The stranger stepped forward, his right hand extended—extended, Aunt Tildy said, in such a generous manner that the recipient might reasonably also expect, if needed, the offer of his socks and under garments.

"John Smith, Sir, at your service! Please allow me to say that I have personally heard William Jennings Bryan speak on many occasions, and his silver words did not once move my heart-strings as did your words on *this* grand day."

Uncle Jack accepted the extended hand with pleasure and the John Smith name without question. He told me once that 98% of Oklahomans were named John Smith, but some humans also carried that name, so the prudent man should not judge in haste.

Aunt Tildy said it was profoundly obvious that John Smith considered a tour of the Battle of the Wilderness Museum, personally guided by the Grand Commander of G.A.R. Post #1000, to be more than he had a right to expect as a mere mortal.

As Lady Auxiliary, Aunt Tildy followed along trying to remember every word and nuance. Uncle Jack introduced his Aide-de-Camp, Lt. Jack O'Hare to Mr. John Smith, and Mr. John Smith acknowledged the bunny with such a bow that Uncle Jack could not but be impressed.

But Aunt Tildy remembered Mr. John Smith looking more carnivorous than social.

Mr. Smith could hardly contain his enthusiasm for the Battle of the Wilderness Museum. He said, "By grab, Sir, the finest museums in the country would be proud to display these relics."

Uncle Jack denied the statement with a sad shake of his head and told Mr. Smith that in the modern condition of museumery, about the only thing anyone was interested in was a fossil fish with another fish in its belly.

Mr. Smith said he had been hearing that same thing more and more in his travels around the country, and that it was a sad state of affairs.

Uncle Jack rubbed his finger along the side of his nose and admitted that he was in personal possession of just such a fish, and if the Lady Auxiliary would consent to having a rope tied around her waist and be lowered into the well, he would be happy to show it.

Mr. Smith said, "By grab, such a piece would be worth a king's ransom!" Aunt Tildy said she knew Uncle Jack began estimating the amount of rope needed to go around her waist and reach the bottom of the well. But Mr. Smith thanked him graciously and said he wouldn't want to put anyone out. He mentioned that, in fact, he had come on business.

Aunt Tildy rocked and pondered. "Mr. Smith's saying he had come on business probably saved us from being a broken family. I never minded the hard-scrabble hungry years, and I never minded the adventure of not knowing what Holy Grail your Uncle Jack was going to chase next. But if I had been asked to descend into a dark well suspended from a worn out old lariat to retrieve a piece of rock with a can of tuna without a label in its belly, I conceivably *might* have minded."

Uncle Jack told the fellow he was always interested in doing business as long as it did not include the Emperor of China, with whom he was no longer on speaking terms.

Mr. Smith said he didn't blame him one bit for that. Chinamen were a segment of people you could not trust, and the danged Emperor was the worst of the litter.

Uncle Jack adjusted his ivory-hilted G.A.R. sword to a

more comfortable hanging and eyed Mr. Smith with a new respect.

"And how do you feel about rattlesnakes, Sir?"

Mr. Smith pulled out what, in a previous incarnation, could have been a handkerchief and dabbed his eyes. Any fool could see that here was a man who had more in his heart than he wanted to talk about concerning rattlesnakes.

"I...I'm afraid I must confess I have not found rattlesnakes to be as reliable as one might have hoped. Forgive me if that's all I say."

Uncle Jack laid a kindly hand on Mr. Smith's shoulder and said, "You don't have to say it. I wonder if you play the bugle?"

Maybe Mr. Smith swallowed a couple of times, and maybe his eyebrows raised a fraction, but he came right back. "I have taken an oath to never play the bugle again."

"By golly," Uncle Jack told him, "So have I. Now, how do you feel about Oklahomans?"

"Oklahomans? Why, sir, I feel I can safely say that I stand four-square with you on that subject."

"Tildy," Uncle Jack cried, "kill that old rooster and set another plate. Mr. Smith will dine with us tonight."

Aunt Tildy told me she was glad when she heard that because Mr. Smith had been eyeing Lt. Jack O'Hare. She was willing to bet if the Lieutenant had been in *his* army, he would have been promoted to *rabbit ragout*.

Aunt Tildy pulled her shawl closer around her bony shoulders. It was not cold, but Tildy was getting old.

"Except for the occasional possibility of ending his career in a pot containing basil and fennel instead of a military funeral with full honors," Aunt Tildy told me, "he was a very fortunate bunny. Well, there I go again! Your Uncle

Jack would not be pleased with me! I can't help it. For all his distinctions and honors and field promotions, to me Lt. Jack O'Hare was still just a cute little bunny."

Conversation at the supper table that evening had rotated mostly around Oklahomans, fossil-finders, and rattlesnakes; there was little good to be said about any of them. Uncle Jack considered them to be of about the same magnitude as the National Commander of the G.A.R.

Mr. John Smith, while shoveling in the food, somehow managed to present an astonished amazement that they could have such similar views. He appeared ready, at any second, to slice his thumb and become a blood brother to Uncle Jack.

After supper Uncle Jack and Mr. John Smith settled themselves on the front porch for a smoke and a belch. Then, with the table ridded and the dishes done, Aunt Tildy ghosted out with a low stool and sat beside Uncle Jack. Lt. Jack O'Hare filled the space between Aunt Tildy and the edge of the porch. He settled and sighed and worked his prosthesis into a comfortable position.

If Mr. John Smith had flaws or failings, impatience was not among them. It was left to Uncle Jack to bring up the subject of business.

"Now, Sir, if I might ask, what business brings you to our humble abode?"

Mr. Smith raised a sausage of a forefinger in supplication for patience, and pranced to his car. He returned, almost cuddling a soft, black leather satchel. The bag was small, but had about it an authority which demanded attention.

Mr. Smith resettled and recomfortabled himself on the porch and rested the bag on the swell of his belly.

"Grand Commander Freeman," he said, "First of all, let

me express my profound gratitude for having been allowed to share in this sacred ceremony today. And I might add that, in my opinion, a grievous wound from a slow-moving cannon ball, even coming some 30 odd years after the war, is no less important than those received in the actual battle.

"Now, as to why I am here. I am here because of the soil of Comanche County.

"...But first I must bore you with my personal history. To see me arrive, disheveled and soiled, in that decrepit carriage, it must be difficult to imagine that I am descended from the hereditary line producing the *Grand Viziers* to the Queens of Albania for hundreds of years.

"This came about because my early ancestor invented asparagus, which soon became the favorite food of the then-Queen. As a reward the Queen granted him and his male descendants, in perpetuity, the right to wear a ring on the ring-toe of the left foot. In retrospect (and doubtless even in the 'spect' of that time) that honor seems like a mighty strange reward for asparagus. But I'll tell you, sir, whatever the Queen of Albania considered a Good Idea, had damn well (excuse my French, Ma'am) better be considered Divine Inspiration by everyone else!

"Mine is a long and noble heritage, and, given that which one of my lineage had every right to expect, I should be living in princely splendor today. But, as you have learned, sir, life is not always fair. I ask for no pity.

"I must admit, I was nearly overwhelmed today because our 'Albanian Potato Rebellion' began on exactly the same day as your 'Battle of the Wilderness!'" His chin sagged toward his breast at the significance and implications of the thought. "The ways of God are far beyond the understanding of mere mortals."

Aunt Tildy told me it was along about this time that Uncle Jack started getting fidgety. She was sure Uncle Jack had as much interest in Albanians and their potatoes as anyone in Comanche County, but much still remained to be said about the Battle of the Wilderness. Perhaps Mr. John Smith sensed this fidgity; perhaps he was just running out of air.

"Oklahomans!" Mr. John Smith suddenly shouted. "Oklahomans and the minions of the Emperor of China! They rebelled my homeland, and in order to bring down the throne, destroyed almost every seed-potato in the kingdom!"

Aunt Tildy told me Uncle Jack sat up so quickly and so straightly that his back popped in more places than it had on their wedding night.

"Oklahomans, you say? Minions of the Emperor of China?" He slapped his leg with such ferocity as to arouse the napping agony of an ankle wounded by a slow-moving cannon ball from the Battle of the Wilderness. "Son-of-a-bitch! I am vindicated, Tildy, I am vindicated! 'The Lord giveth and the Lord taketh away,' and the gol-dang Oklahomans and Chinamen have usurped the Lord's mandate and destroyed nearly every-seed potato in Albania! It's a pure and simple case of *Per Aspera.*"

Mr. Smith saw his chance to expand. I guess if ever a fellow was possessed of expansive capabilities, it was Mr. Smith.

"The Albanian Potato is a far different variety from what most people know, and it is the lifeblood of the Albanian people. Why, an Albanian would sooner have his eyes plucked out than eat an Idaho potato. He would rather see his grandma skinned and boiled than eat a russet. No, sir, the Albanian is mighty finicky when it comes to potatoes! That legume is our national treasure, and it grieves me to the heart that it is now nearly *extinct*."

Aunt Tildy said Mr. John Smith settled back, seeming to sink into himself as if he were subdued by the weight of the world. A nubile young rattlesnake crawled onto his lap and his gentle hand brushed it away.

In a voice as quiet and sincere as God's when he explained to Adam it would be his *butt* if he ate that apple, Mr. John Smith said, "That brings me back to what I started to say about the soil of Comanche County. It is unbelievably similar to that of Albania! Albanian potatoes would prosper and glorify here."

Mr. John Smith convinced about the desperate needs of the current Queen and the people of Albania. He wilted and faded at the future of Albanians and their potatoes. He ecstasized about the future of Comanche County, should anyone be *wise* enough to invest in such potatoes. And sometimes he rainbowed in the pending-glory of the stained glass window for the Lady Auxiliary of Post #1000 of the G.A.R.

Aunt Tildy told me, he "Damn near ascended into heaven" as he opened the soft, black leather satchel and, with the exuberance of giving birth to twins, presented the last two Albanian seed-potatoes: the last breeding stock, the last hope for Albania.

"The Royal Albanian Potato!"

Aunt Tildy said these Royal Albanian Potatoes maybe looked Albanian, but they did not look royal. Still, she said, she was not the one to judge.

"As potatoes," she said, "they looked soft and sorrowful. They had sprouted, with long, whitish-green sprouts. I wouldn't have fed them to the pigs, if we had had any—which we didn't."

Uncle Jack, on the other hand, had stopped rocking and

was leaning forward nearly snout to snout with Mr. John Smith. It was Aunt Tildy's opinion that being in the presence of the last of the Royal Albanian seed-potatoes was a treasure Uncle Jack was storing away in his mind and heart like the memory of his grandma.

Mr. Smith pointed out the sprouts first off. He said it was a manifestation of their eagerness to breed and reproduce.

"Now, this one," and Mr. Smith proudly lifted the one in his left hand, "is 'Ignatius,' the stallion of the Albanian potato—the 'stud spud,' if you will. He is aptly named because the word 'Ignatius' comes down from the Greek and the Latin and means 'fiery.'"

Aunt Tildy kindly and generously remembered old "Ignatius" as maybe, just perhaps, having once been "fiery," but not within the life span of her mama or grandma.

"This proud lady," Mr. Smith continued, "I call 'Queenie.' He raised the potato in his right hand carefully so as not to disturb her, "Although her full name is 'Queen of the Nile.' As I am sure you are aware, Grand Commander, the Nile is our sacred river in Albania. It flows in a westerly direction from the mountains, across the grassy savanna, and even unto the distant sea. And in its long journey, it, in better times, nourished the Royal Albanian Potato which, in turn, nourished Albania. Well, Sir, the beautiful Nile still flows through Albania, but because of the Oklahomans and the Emperor of China, thousands of gentle Albanians are dropping like flies from starvation."

Aunt Tildy said she had wished and wished that this potato-man would just shut his mouth. She could read the subtle signs which told her that Uncle Jack was not going to put up with much damn more abuse to the poor Albanians.

He had, without thinking, pulled his smooth-oiled

revolver from his belt and was fondling it dangerously on his lap. As Mr. John Smith nodded his head approvingly, and not quite under his breath muttered, "Oklahomans, Chinamen," Uncle Jack's knuckles whitened on the grip of his Smith and Wesson.

"Sir," Uncle Jack said, "this is intolerable! G.A.R. Post #1000 will do what it can. How can we help?"

Mr. John Smith leaned even closer and whispered, "Grow these potatoes! You will save the good people of Albania and make your fortune at the same time."

"We will do it! Yes, sir, by grab, we will do it!" Uncle Jack reached for the potatoes, but the potatoes retreated! And the further Uncle Jack reached, the further the potatoes retreated.

Mr. John Smith looked as if it pained him to his gizzard to have to say so, but eventually he was able to explain that in order to show good faith on both sides, he would give Uncle Jack the potatoes when Uncle Jack gave him $13. Uncle Jack, whose glazed eyes could only see Albanians dropping like flies for want of a Royal Potato, reached for his wallet.

It was at this time, Aunt Tildy told me, that Lt. Jack O'Hare, who had been sitting quietly as behooves a subordinate officer, risked a court martial and made his statement concerning the Albanian Potato Salesman.

"That little old jack rabbit," Aunt Tildy said, "using his straight-grained cedar prosthesis as a sort of club, just thonked the living bejesus out of your Great Uncle Jack's Battle-of-the-Wilderness-cannon-ball-wounded ankle!"

Uncle Jack came out of that chair with a *whoop*. The revolver, still in his white-knuckled hand, sent two bullets through the floor and one bullet close enough to Mr.

Smith's head to remind him of a previously-made appointment.

He departed with a speed which would belie our preconceived notions pertaining to the agility of a portly man. The last surviving Royal Albanian Potato breeding stock were smashed as flat as Morgan dollars under his white-spatted brogans.

The ankle-thonk and the cracks of the revolver caused Uncle Jack's eyes to de-glaze. He uncharacteristically admitted that he had almost been duped, and added Albanians to his growing list: Oklahomans, Chinamen, rattlesnakes *and* Albanians. All faced a bleak future if Uncle Jack ever became God.

With the scales fallen from his eyes, the Grand Commander granted Lt. Jack O'Hare his captaincy on the spot.

17

A New Prosthesis

Having once admitted to being mesmerized nearly to the point of bamboozlement, Uncle Jack never mentioned Mr. Smith again. But wallowing in embarrassment was not Uncle Jack's style, although Aunt Tildy told me he could appreciate that quality in other people.

So the days passed and the nights passed, and if Aunt Tildy ever, in her mind, compared the brain power of her husband to the brain power of a jack rabbit, she never mentioned it to me. However, it nagged at Aunt Tildy how close Uncle Jack had come to being taken in by the smooth-talking Albanian potato man. So it was no coincidence that the Lady Auxiliary of Post # 1000 started to take a serious interest in improving Capt. Jack O'Hare's life and career.

For one thing, it had become obvious that the cedar prosthesis, no matter how free from knots, no matter how straight of grain, was not a perfect fit. Aunt Tildy believed that there was no Surgeon General in any G.A.R. Post in America who could have done a better job of fitting a wooden leg to a rabbit than had my own Uncle Jack. Still, it really did not work well because the prosthesis was not hinged at the ankle.

"Could he hop?" I asked.

"Of course he could hop," Aunt Tildy said. "He hopped with a weary dignity, like an English officer with a game leg, home from the Boer War."

I pondered that and let it pass. Aunt Tildy was getting old.

So the Lady Auxiliary made it her business to coax and threaten and badger until Uncle Jack found another piece of clear cedar, sharpened his pocket knife, and sat down on the front porch to try again.

He placed the Captain on a small table in front of him and set about to calculate the proper dimensions of the new prosthesis. Uncle Jack explained that the height, the length, and the angle at which the paw hit the ground had to all be ciphered in, lest the Captain list to starboard or to port, lest he be pitched forward on his bunny nose or bumped along on his bunny butt. Of course, Uncle Jack would never called the Captain a bunny; those were Aunt Tildy's words.

Aunt Tildy said it was done pretty much "by guess and by gosh," because "a jack rabbit, no matter how docile and how patient, is a difficult commodity to measure." On top of that, despite his own innate dignity and the dignity of his rank, Captain Jack O'Hare was hopelessly ticklish.

The carving and fitting took several days, but Aunt Tildy declared the new prosthesis to be a "marvel of engineering and a sight to behold." The ankle joint took the form of a mortise and tenon. Two pieces of flat spring from a Seth Thomas clock were attached to cantilevered projections on the upper leg, one in front and one in back. The springs pressed opposing cams carved on the foot, causing it to always return to the normal, paw-flat-on-the-ground position. Aunt Tildy said, "The thing was a little spooky; it seemed almost alive."

Uncle Jack painted the new prosthesis with the same paint he had used on the little flags in the Battle of the Wilderness Museum: red, white and green (because he didn't have any blue). Aunt Tildy secretly wondered if the garishness of the new foot and leg would cause embarrassment to the Captain, but she was loath to question a decision of the Surgeon General.

The big day finally arrived, and Aunt Tildy remembered it clearly. The paint was dry, and soft new leather straps with old shoe buckles had been attached. Aunt Tildy pondered. "It looked like nothing I ever saw," she said. "I figure some folks might consider it a sort of work of art, and some folks might just want to pull a gun and shoot it on sight as an affront to nature.

"In retrospect, I think it might have been better if the strapping-on had been done with only the surgeon and the amputee in attendance. But that was not your Uncle Jack's style. He assembled as many members of G.A.R. Post #1000 as he could find and donned his Grand Commander-Surgeon General uniform and sword with the ivory hilt."

Captain Jack O'Hare appeared apprehensively eager as Uncle Jack approached with the new prosthesis. The Captain braced and steadied himself as the old one was removed. Aunt Tildy said he "done well."

"Done well, that is, until one of his ticklish fits came over him. When your Uncle Jack went to attach the new leg with the hinged and cantilevered spring-loaded foot, the Captain just plain collapsed into a little heap of bunny giggles and meeps. It was all very unmilitary-like. Jack had to use his sternest voice to bring the Captain to attention and make him hold still until the thing was strapped on. The whole affair put a serious strain on the dignity of G.A.R.

Post #1000.

"But when everything was in place and secure, Jack placed the Captain on the ground, and it was an almost-glorious moment. Your Uncle Jack had miscalculated the ratio of relationship as to clock-spring-to-rabbit, and in ten hops the Captain had veered about thirteen degrees off course. But there was no disaster. The foot went *clack-clickety* at every hop, which added a sort of military cadence and pleased the Captain immensely. The extra lift on one side gave him a certain élan which I had not noticed he lacked.

"After three circles around the yard, Captain Jack O'Hare had corrected his ambulatory windage, and when he presented himself before the Grand Commander, he came not as a ticklish bunny, but as a swaggery-bragery Prussian."

Aunt Tildy said Uncle Jack was pleased beyond redemption and graciously awarded himself a promotion to *Grand* Surgeon General.

18

Uncle Jack Gets Snake-Bit

Uncle Jack died on June 18, 1913.

That was the *first time* he died, so he remembered it pretty well. (He never mentioned the last time—at least not to me).

In all the years the family lived on the hereditary Birthing and Dying Grounds of the little massasauga rattlesnakes, Uncle Jack was the only one ever bitten. He said it was his fault and his fault alone, because he had inadvertently trod upon a very sensitive portion of a young adult male rattlesnake who was just out looking for a good time and was not out to have any very sensitive portion of himself trod upon.

It came about in this way:

Either despite of or because of Uncle Jack's attention being diverted into other pursuits, his herd of beef cattle had prospered unbelievably.

Aunt Tildy would attest to the fact that Uncle Jack spent an inordinate amount of time keeping Mr. Henry Spickelmeir's father's Battle of the Wilderness bugle and Battle of the Wilderness right brogan polished—to the extent that she feared they would wear from thin to nothing.

And the carving, painting and fitting of an articulated prosthesis for a commissioned jack rabbit also took a lot of Uncle Jack's time. It was Aunt Tildy's opinion that had not the bulls and the cows had a natural propensity for acting like bulls and cows, the ranch would have "flat gone to hell."

But they multiplied. Like rattlesnakes and cockleburs, they multiplied. It's a tribute to Aunt Tildy's loyalty as a wife that she never actually said that the more Uncle Jack stayed out of the way, the better things seemed to work.

Uncle Jack's "dying story" was honed down to a pretty fine edge. It always included Genesis 3:1: "Now the serpent was more subtle than any beast of the field which the Lord God had made."

"But," he would point out, (Uncle Jack, not God) "that garden of Eden serpent was most likely a serpent who had not had his very sensitive parts stepped on."

Because the cattle herd increased much faster than Royal Albanian Potatoes, Uncle Jack decided that, like a real cattle baron, he should have his own brand. For several days the Battle of the Wilderness bugle and the Battle of the Wilderness brogan were neither polished nor dusted.

Uncle Jack sat at the kitchen table sketching designs for

a brand which would demand respect and bring suitable dignity to the ranch.

The "Bar F" (for Freeman) with an encirclement of entwining rattlesnakes was rejected because Uncle Jack, quite rightly, concluded that a rattlesnake image would not reproduce well burned into the hide of a steer. The "Bar F" with cockleburs rampant, was discarded as too frivolous. Uncle Jack said it was early morning of the third day when he finally found the perfect brand: a "Bar F" crowning a cow-with-another-cow-in-its-belly.

Aunt Tildy said Uncle Jack's excitement was palpable as he... No, what she *really* said was, "Your Uncle Jack was about ready to soil his undergarments as he mounted his horse and took the sketch over to Coldwater to the blacksmith."

If the branding-iron-making blacksmith was struck dumb with the beauty and artistry of Uncle Jack's design, it was never mentioned in my presence. But Uncle Jack was exuberant upon arriving home. In his exuberance, he carelessly swung down off his horse and trod on a sensitive region of an adult male massasauga.

It was a mystery to me how that little rattlesnake could reach high enough to bite above the height of the boots Uncle Jack always wore. Uncle Jack guessed that the snake had extra motivation because of the area on which he was accidentally trodden.

Aunt Tildy said that even though she was a female, she could understand the motivation. However, in her opinion, Uncle Jack may not have completely forgiven the rattlesnakes for deserting him when he was trying to master the nuances of the Battle of the Wilderness bugle, so she was not one-hundred percent convinced that the trodding was entirely accidental.

Uncle Jack said that in all honesty he did not realize he had been bitten until he noticed that the snake had a pained grin on its face and was nodding its head up and down in a "yes" motion, calling his attention to the fact.

Aunt Tildy said when she heard Uncle Jack *whooping* his way towards the house she, understandably, assumed that the Oklahomans had come back for another baseball game. Remembering the pleasure one of the Oklahoma players had derived from eating her home-made lye soap—and being the good hostess that she was—Aunt Tildy started to assemble her soap making fixings.

It was amid this well-intended flurry that Uncle Jack burst through the back door announcing that he had just received his death wound from a serpent who was not, in any way shape nor form, as subtle as he had been led to believe from reading Genesis 3:1.

Aunt Tildy had by this time got herself into a soap-making mode and her power of concentration was pretty much utilized. She told him that there was still a piece of soap left if he felt the need of a bath.

"Gol-dang it woman," Uncle Jack exclaimed, "I am snake-bit unto extinction, and you want me to take a bath? You can bathe me when my stiff and suppurated body lies cold and naked on the kitchen table!"

Aunt Tildy said that all Uncle Jack's ranting had just about made her give up making soap. By the time Uncle Jack (minus his trousers) was laid out on the bed, his knee joint had already started to swell badly. Aunt Tildy told me the knee turned about as green as a paw-paw. Then she pondered a while and told me it was really more the color of an avocado, but avocados had not yet been invented—so how was she to know?

Uncle Jack's fever began raising, and he started talking a steady line of jibberish. He begged her to send for a priest although he had never before shown the slightest inclination toward the Romish persuasion. His mind calcified on Extreme Unction, not knowing or caring if Extreme Unction was delivered from a hypodermic needle or an honest shot glass. He was lucid enough to tell her he would require at least a pint of it, because being snake-bit was a dreadful thing. Aunt Tildy said, "For crying out loud, Jack!"

Captain Jack O'Hare hunkered by the sick bed in silence, his little whiskers alternately drooping in sadness and then bristling in anger. Aunt Tildy said that about every fifteen minutes he hopped outside and with his red, white and green double-spring-loaded articulated prosthesis, thonked the living bejesus out of any rattlesnake that crossed his path.

The carnage was immense.

As she told me the story Uncle Jack raised his hairy-backed old hand to shut off her prattling. "The point is," he reminded us, "I died!"

"The point is," Aunt Tildy reminded us, "Bull hocky!"

"No, sir," he declared, "I was dead as Kelsey's nuts!"

I will mention at this point that I have searched my books for any mention of this "Kelsey" and his unfortunate affliction, to no avail.

"I remember looking down through a long tunnel which was big enough to hold thirteen boxcar loads of gold nuggets," Uncle Jack told us. And there at the end, it was all bright, but with little stars going around and up and down and doing dipsy-doodles. And I remember thinking, goldang, it is unusual to see stars at high-noon.

"It is a contrary-to-fact assumption that in your last minute, your whole life flashes before your eyes. My last thought was 'This is the absolute most pure and simple manifestation *of Ad Astra Per Aspera* I am ever likely to witness!' Those stars were the *Astras,* and that damn rattlesnake was the *Aspera!* And I fell into considering the coincidence of the fact that the first part of "*Aspera"* was "asp." And, just like with old Cleopatra, I was dead because of a serpent, even though mine was a just-above-the-knee-bite and hers was a bosom-bite. I seemed to be filled with the wisdom of the ages.

"Anyway, there at the end of the tunnel in that bright light, I beheld my mama and my daddy and my oldest brother, Richard. Richard had never advanced beyond the spermatozoa stage—and so not even my mother ever knew about him. But I seemed to recognize him, and they were all beckoning at me to come on through.

Old Richard stuck two fingers up to his teeth and gave a whistle and waved his arm to let me know that his side of the tunnel was the only sensible side to be on. But I had not just fallen off the turnip wagon! I had survived the machinations of the Emperor of China and a son-of-a-bitching Albanian potato salesman, and I was damn sure not going to be suckered in by a spermatozoa named Richard.

Aunt Tildy shook her head as if searching for a stronger expletive. Then, as if admitting her poor education and her poor vocabulary, she just reminded us, "Bull hockey."

"Well," Uncle Jack ignored, "it was just when I had started seeking an alternative route to crawling through that danged tunnel into heaven that I was struck dead-center on my snake-bit leg, struck without pity or mercy, struck by a pain eleven times worse than having a head blown off at the

Battle of the Wilderness, and an *infinity* worse than losing a brogan.

"Your Aunt Tildy, who is 1/16 part witch, had concocted a poultice out of God only knows what. Without pity or mercy she slapped it on my leg and set about to draw out the snake poison."

Uncle Jack sat there, as was his habit when he told me about the old days, stropping his pocket knife on the upper end of his boot.

"I expect that whatever she put in that poultice, it was mostly turnips because I smelled of turnips for about the next 18 months. But it worked. That starry tunnel and my mama and my daddy and brother, Spermatozoa Richard, just sort of passed into oblivion, and I woke up completely normal."

"Bull hocky," Aunt Tildy told the porch roof.

"No, sir," Uncle Jack said, "I rose up from the dead just like old Lazarus—except my hair had turned completely white and gotten so curly that the women could scarce keep their hands off me and..."

Aunt Tildy stood up so quickly her poor old knees popped. She poured her last few drops of lemonade right on top of Uncle Jack's head. "Double bull hocky," she told him.

He didn't even shoot her. He just winked at me as the screen door slammed behind her and said, "Ain't she somethin'?"

19

Enough Is Too Much

Aunt Tildy said that the death bite from the massasauga, the tunnel with the light, and the unconceived, unknown-about (and therefore unremorsed) elder brother, Spermatozoa Richard, had cast Uncle Jack into a frame of mind which pulled his thoughts into the sphere of mortality.

In a train of thought which was still pretty-well skewed by massasauga juice, he explained that he had been negligent in the preparation for his demise and had procured neither coffin nor sarcophagus. It was a situation which he determined to remedy as soon as he was up and around again.

Maybe Aunt Tildy made a mental note to add sarcophagus to her shopping list for the next time they went to Coldwater, but she mostly preferred to consider one thing at a time and puzzle over it until she understood it.

"I asked your Uncle Jack just what, exactly, was a 'Spermatozoa Richard,'" she told me. "He said they were so tiny you scarce could see them, and they were squiggley as all get-out. He said that it was extremely unusual for one to put his fingers to his teeth and whistle—and even more unusual for one to be named 'Richard.'

"Your Uncle Jack was well-read," Aunt Tildy said. "Most of what I know about the world I learned from him. For instance, he said that when you meet your average spermatozoa, you will find him named 'Earl.' Jack said he had read about one or two named 'Ralph.' About, maybe, three were called 'Swede.' One, over in Barton County, was named 'Homer,' and one passed as 'Rastus.' So, for the most part and as a general rule, you could not go far wrong addressing a spermatozoa as 'Earl.'

"Now, in all that time when your Uncle was recuperating, Captain Jack O'Hare was rarely more than five feet away. He *clack-clickateed* on his double-cantilevered-spring-loaded-articulated-clear-grain-cedar-red-white-and-green prosthesis up and down the warped cottonwood-planked bedroom floor. I guess, in his little bunny heart, he could feel the conflict and the loss of directional bearing which was manifesting itself in Jack's inner-most being in regard to having a spermatozoa brother named Richard.

"Your Uncle Jack figured that the odds of having a spermatozoa brother named Richard were about four-million-point-six-ought-point-eight to one. Well, all of those oughts and all of those points just gave me a severe headache, so I lay down on the fainting couch. I did not have the leisure to faint, however, because Jack hollered in and told me to consider a spermatozoa as looking like a centipede.

"So I lay there on that fainting couch considering a centipede with a forehead such as a Freeman might have and a nose like a Freeman might have, and my headache did not find a great deal of relief. Learning that I had an almost brother-in-law who resembled a centipede was not a prospect to dwell on.

"Throughout the years, I had met a few of your Uncle Jack's family. As I lay there, I squinted the eyes of my mind down to where the light barely squiggled through. I could see my mother-in-law, your Uncle Jack's mama. Suddenly, it made perfect and absolute sense. The centipedical denomination came from the *McIntire* side of the family.

"So I lay there, giggling a little, almost wishing the poor old soul were still alive so I could tell her I had finally figured out what she reminded me of. But I'll tell you, the pleasure of that possibility did not extend to the point where I actually wished her back alive. I know it is an unchristian thought, and I may roast in Hell for even thinking it, but I never, ever, was as fond of your Uncle Jack's mother as when she finally passed on.

"Well, about then Jack seemed to suffer a relapse because he shouted for me to bring him his G.A.R. sword. He said that the Emperor of China had played fast and loose with this native Kansan one time too many, and that he (The Emperor of China) was about to die a horrible death.

"I hollered back that, in case he had not heard, Mr. Lincoln had freed the slaves and so he could get his own damn sword.

He hollered back, 'Gol-dang it, woman!'

I hollered back, 'I will see that *gol-dang it*, and raise you five.'

"He muttered something, but God was in the act of granting me relief and respite in the form of me imagining my mother-in-law as a centipede. The last thing I heard as I slipped into blissful oblivion was the Captain's *clack-click-ating* and the chickens raising 'Hail Columbia' in the back-yard."

20

Sarcophagus-Shopping in Coldwater

"It was on a Thursday."

Aunt Tildy was sure it had been on a Thursday. But, by this time, months meant nothing to her, and the years had melded together like a bean salad on its fifth day.

She had found the picture of Grant's Tomb on the table when she started to set out breakfast, and she was wise enough to know a bad omen when she found one—especially when the omen was where the platter of bacon was supposed to go.

Uncle Jack had recovered from death better than most people. He credited Aunt Tildy's poultice, but Aunt Tildy told me it was due to "old Satan not laying in an adequate supply of anthricite coal to roast such a mean old rascal."

Aunt Tildy said the Board of Directors of the Forces of Evil had been forced to call an emergency meeting at the time of Uncle Jack's demise. They had called old Satan in and given him a mild rebuke for his lack of preparedness, and old Satan just stood there, shamefaced and chagrined, lightly fingering a nasty burn just below his elbow and scratching simple designs with his cloven hooves in a light dusting of ashes.

"Then, somebody, I believe it was Attila the Hun, spoke up and said, 'Hell, he'll be back eventually!'

"Well, before they could catch themselves, a large majority of the Board members blurted out, '*Amen* to that!' Which, of course, was a poor choice of words in that part of the country.

"A quick vote was held with none of the voters meeting the eyes of the other voters, and your Uncle Jack was sent back to the world of the living until such time as they could be prepared for him."

Uncle Jack's recent mention of coffins and sarcophagi, added to her finding of a fine lithograph of Grant's Tomb where the bacon was supposed to be placed—was a signal and a portent to Aunt Tildy. Life in Comanche County was about to change again, and there was not the slightest reason to imagine it might be a change for the better.

Uncle Jack pulled the buckboard up to the front steps, Aunt Tildy, lifting her skirts modestly, descended the porch steps with a *regality* which I doubt Queen Victoria could have bettered. But Queen Victoria was probably never granted the pleasure and joy of driving off to Coldwater, Kansas with a long shopping list and a purse full of cattle-begotten money.

Captain Jack O'Hare stood at the top of the porch steps, his double-spring-loaded prosthesis thonking ominously on the wooden planks. It was Aunt Tildy's opinion that if any roving bands of marauders tried to invade the ranch, the Captain would have "thonked" them until they rued that day.

Aunt Tildy told me she remembered that morning pretty well. "It was a Thursday morning," she repeated, "a spring morning when you could smell the green in the air, with maybe a hint of sage." She said the horse had started out a little skitterish, but Uncle Jack had used that *suckery-clickery* sound of his, which seemed to explain to most horses just who was in charge and who was not.

Aunt Tildy loved Comanche County, but she figured God had created it when He was still a teenager. The soil was red as red could possibly be in one spot, and then it was black in another. It was red dust, or red mud. It was black dust, or black mud. It was bright green and dark green, with bees and bugs thrown in at no extra cost. It was as flat as flat could possibly be, and then, it reared up and, look out! It was sharp points and rounded off points and low cliffs.

"And there we were, going to Coldwater in that old buckboard, Aunt Tildy said. "Maybe your Uncle Jack never looked so good to me. He was still a little wan and a little gaunt from being snake-bit above the boot, but that droopy old mustache glistened with little sparkles of red in it here and there, and some of the sparkle had come back into his eyes.

"I truly do not believe that Jack smelled a smell or saw a flower on that whole trip. No, sir, he was completely consumed with the idea of finding himself a sarcophagus. It wasn't a morbid thing. He was excited as a Christmas kid.

"The Sears and Roebuck catalog, where one might reasonably expect to find a good, moderately-priced sarcophagus, had been no help at all," Aunt Tildy said. "But Jack was not discouraged. He said he had been caught dead without a sarcophagus once, and he dang sure was not going to let it happen again!

"We, neither one of us, ever mentioned the fine lithograph of Grant's Tomb which was laid where the bacon was supposed to be. I believe he would have enjoyed having a similar edifice, but it is my thought that your Uncle Jack preferred the sound of 'sarcophagus' to 'tomb.' 'Tomb' was just not enough of a word for Jack.

"So we bumped along that old road toward Coldwater, and Jack extolled and explained the finer points of sarcophagi. He said they come in a variety of shapes and sizes, but what he had in mind was just a simple, big old piece of rock which had been hollowed out like a bathtub. He said the lid alone on a sarcophagus would weigh about a ton and, traditionally, it took at least six slaves just to put on the lid. As gently and as tactfully as I could, I asked him when he had last conducted a head count of our slaves.

"He said, 'Damnation! ...Well, I expect that in a town the size of Coldwater it will be hard to find a sarcophagus with a lid weighing less than a ton, but I will do the best I can.'

"I put my arm around that old snake-bit, back-from-the-dead rascal and told him if he happened on to a sarcophagus built for two, that would be just fine with me."

So, as I understand it, Aunt Tildy took her list of staple goods into the store, and Uncle Jack went on down the street pondering as to how he might broach the subject of sarcophagi without sending the prices skyrocketing.

Walt Bosco was the first fellow he met, and that was fine with Uncle Jack. Walt was a good old boy, and he pretty much knew what was going on around Coldwater. However, as many may have found from their own experiences, there is an inherent difficulty in introducing sarcophagi into a conversation in Coldwater.

As Aunt Tildy heard it from Uncle Jack and told it to me, Walt Bosco gave Uncle Jack a long, slow wink and allowed as how Uncle Jack was a regular fellow and surely could be trusted. He told Uncle Jack that he had heard there was a certain individual up in Kiowa County who occasionally ran off a gallon or two of "skarfigi" for his own use and could sometimes be persuaded to share it with the needy.

Uncle Jack thanked him for his trust and information, then told Walt that if he ever got up that way, he would bring him a little something for his trouble.

Aunt Tildy said it was at this point Uncle Jack realized he was just wasting his time with people like Walt Bosco. So he walked south and entered Adolph Himmelspiegel's Furniture and Undertaking Establishment.

That was where Aunt Tildy caught up with him. She noticed old Deafy Himmelspiegel had a sign on the front of the building which proclaimed the establishment to be the "Mirror of Heaven," and she told me that it might well have been, but it did not manifest itself to her in that regard.

It turned out that Aunt Tildy entered the "Mirror of Heaven" about two minutes after Uncle Jack. Old Deafy Himmelspiegel was wiping the sweat off his brow because he had just been building a coffin for Louise Sprinkle, who had died of shock and heartbreak because her beloved had been scrunched to death between two boxcars. Aunt Tildy said it was just bull hocky, because everybody except

Louise Sprinkle knew that he had not, in reality, been *her* beloved.

It was Aunt Tildy's opinion that, by the time she arrived, Uncle Jack had already explained his mission and his need to Deafy Himmelspiegel about three times, and Deafy Himmelspiegel was probably doing the best he could to hear and understand. But there stood Uncle Jack, nearing exasperation, shouting, "Sarcophagus! Gol-dang it, Sarcophagus!"

Old Deafy Himmelspiegel, assuming that the dust from Louise Sprinkle's coffin had gotten up Uncle Jack's nose, leaned into Uncle Jack's face and shouted, "Gesundheit! I haf twice, already, Gott-dang it, told you, Gesundheit!"

Uncle Jack stomped out of the "Mirror of Heaven" declaring that if there were a more uninformed, downright ignorant group of citizens in any county seat in Kansas, he would be very much surprised. He was willing to bet that up north in Topeka a fellow could not walk ten feet without tripping over a sarcophagus.

On the way back home Aunt Tildy queried Uncle Jack about when he figured was the last time he had heard of anyone actually using a sarcophagus. Uncle Jack pondered that, and then told her as near as he could remember it had been Jesus, or maybe Lazarus.

"Where," Aunt Tildy asked, "do you reckon he got it?"

Uncle Jack communioned his leg up against hers and said, "Most likely Wichita, honey, or maybe Medicine Lodge."

21

A Welcoming Home

That old buckboard rattled and bumped its way up the lane to home, and home was exactly where they most wanted to be. It was a far piece from home to Coldwater, and about twice as far back. They were both tired and dusty. Uncle Jack, Aunt Tildy said, "was still not quite his-self from the bite."

They had enough staple goods to see them through for a while. But the old blankets which Uncle Jack had brought along to protect his sarcophagus from dents and scratches lay in the back of the buckboard, still folded, as a testament to the fact that Comanche County had a ways to go to catch up with civilization.

In the telling of what followed, Uncle Jack and Aunt Tildy were, for once, mostly in agreement. Their recollections differed on the details, but the main fact was beyond dispute.

Captain Jack O'Hare had coerced all or most of the chickens into a rough semblance of a military formation across the front porch as a welcome home committee.

Uncle Jack told me, "anytime one of those birds stepped out of line they got thonked in the tail feathers by a spring-loaded prosthesis."

Aunt Tildy said she should have known something was going on a few days earlier when she heard the Captain raising "Hail Columbia" in the chicken house. "But that was when Jack was lying snake-bit, without his pants, and my soap-making ingredients were being left unattended. For all anybody cared, the whole family could have been consumed by dirt and filth."

"The point is," Uncle Jack said, "it was plain to see that Captain O'Hare had been putting those chickens through their paces. From the way the old rooster stood a little off to one side and glared with his googley eyes, I judged the Captain had made him a Sergeant."

Uncle Jack chuckled, but Aunt Tildy bristled. "I told your uncle that it might look cute and clever to him, but to me it was a pure and simple omen. I told him that that jack rabbit had been bit by a Napoleon bug, and he had better be stopped now—before he set out to conquer the world."

"But, Tildy," Uncle Jack reasoned, "Omens are practically never the color of jack rabbits. They are mostly a sort of a weak green."

"Have pity on me, Lord! Jack Freeman, I have seen a wagon load of omens, and in my entire life I have only seen one which was 'weak green.' No, sir, omens come in all colors of the rainbow. Why, when I was still a girl in Iway I saw one which was of the McAlister tartan," Aunt Tildy said.

Then she pondered. "I guess my favorite omens are the ones which are variegated, like the embroidery work on the pillowslips which Grandma gave us for our wedding. But portents? Yes, I will agree that portents are most often a subtle…"

"By the blisters on God's aching feet, Tildy!" Uncle Jack roared, "Are we going spend the night talking about the wonders of variegated, embroidered pillowslips? Might we, please, get around to telling Max about the only time in recorded history when a jack rabbit displayed the intelligence and leadership to make a line of dumb Rhode Island Reds stand in a reasonably straight line on a front porch?"

Aunt Tildy gave him a pitying look, turned her gaze from Uncle Jack and put it on me. "One of them was an Orpington," she told me. "But the other hens pecked her to death."

"… the smartest rabbit who ever hopped on the face of the earth!" Uncle Jack tapped the ashes from his pipe, blew out the dottle and the gurgley stuff, and ambled toward the outhouse.

"Orpington," Aunt Tildy told me. "One of them was an Orpington."

22

Caught in a Comanche County Piss-Cutter

July and I arrived in Comanche County for our regular visits on the same day. I think that summer I was about nine years old. I came with my brown cardboard suitcase, and July came with its cheeks puffed out with wind. School had been out long enough for my parents to begin having thoughts as to how selfish they were to keep me all to themselves. It was a two-way street, as most streets are.

It is pure conjecture on my part, but I have the distinct feeling that if Uncle Jack and Aunt Tildy had not been ready to welcome me, my folks would have shared me with anybody available, be it in Ogden, Utah or Elk Hocky, Montana.

The train eased into Coldwater, granting its blessing with a smell of coal smoke and hissing, oily steam.

And there stood Uncle Jack. He was even taller than I remembered, and he was wearing his low-slung-tied-down Smith and Wesson. I knew he had worn it for me. (Aunt Tildy had told me last summer that it had been ever-so-long since Uncle Jack had shot anyone.)

He swooped me up so easily I might as well have been hollow. He had forgotten—or didn't care—that I was nearly nine. He smelled like horse sweat and leather and tobacco, with perhaps a hint of the delicate aroma of the local distillate, *Comanche County Panther Piss*. All rolled into one, it was the best smell in the world.

I didn't care that he hugged me to him like I was a girl. It didn't last long. Then he held me out at arm's length, and his eyes glittered right into mine. "Howdy, Stranger," he said.

I wanted to reach out with just one finger and touch his Smith and Wesson. Uncle Jack had been right, even though he had not meant it that way. The winter months had gone by, and I *was* a sort of stranger.

Anyway, Uncle Jack sprang onto that horse and, with a hairy paw, pulled me and my suitcase up behind him. We were off at a gallop before I could adjust my trousers to where they would probably not saw me in two.

"You gotta new horse," I shouted, "What's his name?"

"Dobbin," he hollered back. We headed east, leaving Coldwater in a cloud of dust.

"Hows come you name every horse you get Dobbin?" The wind was picking up quickly and surprise splats of rain were beginning to pelt us. The Coldwater dust seemed to be chasing us and turning into mud-balls.

It didn't take Uncle Jack half a minute to adjust his

windage to fit the topic of Dobbin naming. "It's not my doing. It's Biblical."

I couldn't see Uncle Jack's face, but by the shake of his head, I could imagine his forlorn expression.

The sprinkles and the wind slacked off for a moment. Uncle Jack kept shouting, "I can see that your education has suffered woefully while you have been away. We must do a lot of Bible reading while you're here.

"Dobbin comes from the book of the Pharisees 1:11: 'And the beast shall be of four legs, and upon his back shall he convey a handsome warrior and a kid with a brown cardboard suitcase. And his name shall be called Dobbin and Dobbin shall be his name.'"

I guess I grinned until I might have ruptured my appendix.

"Ad Astra Per Aspera," I piped in his ear.

"Gol-dang right!" He bellowed. He dredged up a loud and frightful *whoop* from his long-ago cowboy days, pulled out his Smith and Wesson, and fired off three rounds into the belly of the ugly black cloud which had snuck up unbeknownst from our backside.

I knew I was no longer a stranger.

Much later, during my days at the University, I described what happened next to learned professors, people who claimed to understand weather patterns and clouds. I discussed it with theologians, and late one night, in desperation, I discussed it with a fellow who had a government grant to study how many electric eels it would take to light all of the sixty-watt bulbs in Corry, Pennsylvania.

I learned a lot from that experience. Oh, I got laughed at—a lot. But along the way I gained the understanding that folks, even those with advanced degrees, who have never endured being under an ugly black cloud which has just had three rounds of Smith and Wesson exuberance launched into its roily underbelly, are a different breed of cat from those who have.

What happened was this: the rain had let up for about three-quarters of a mile, and I figured it was about over. But then I cocked my head around to where I could see back over my shoulder, and... Oh, my! That black cloud was still there. It was *more* than there. Black was all there was— black, and seven miles of ominous. I don't really expect anyone to believe this, especially anyone who has an advanced degree nailed to their wall, but it was as if that old black cloud had just been holding off, waiting for a kid with a brown cardboard suitcase to turn around and see it.

The temperature dropped what I would now call "precipitously." Years later, when I asked Aunt Tildy if she thought the temperature had dropped precipitously that day, she told me that, at that time, only folks above Reno County used that word on a regular basis. She said she had heard that some of the aristocrats up at the Normal School at Emporia bandied the word around, but by and large and for the most part, *they* thought it meant "strawberry parfait."

So I queried Aunt Tildy as to how, at that time, one might reasonably and accurately describe a sudden and abrupt drop in the temperature about three or four miles east of Coldwater. She said, "Tell them it dropped like 'a bat out of Hell!'"

The temperature dropped like a bat out of Hell.

What had been perhaps a shade too warm soon became about twelve shades too cold. Surprisingly, there were still a few dry patches of ground which the wind found, and whipped red dust all around us like a bat out of Hell. The rain again began falling in a deceptively soft way. Soon, little pellets of dust-mixed ice started peppering down on us. At first it was sort of pleasant, but I guess that old black cloud was just getting in a little practice.

As the red hail kept coming, the cloud hung lower and lower, and old Dobbin, getting pelted with undeserved abuse, started getting skittish. Uncle Jack hollered for me to slide off, and I did. He swung down and hooked his thumb somewhere near Dobbin's bridle-bit and rubbed Dobbin's nose. "There, there," he told him.

Let me insert right here that I have spent many hours pondering as to how anyone might think the words, "There, there," could improve a disastrous situation. Should I get my finger smashed in the door of a Plymouth sedan, I would, most likely consider the words, "there, there," woefully inadequate.

As soon as I finish this story about Comanche County, it is my intent to create a chart showing the relative power of words. For instance, "bull hocky" will be in the first echelon and "there, there" will be down at about 712. I modestly anticipate being offered of an honorary Ph.D. for my work on that chart, which I shall graciously decline because, until somebody steps forward and publicly apologies for not at least *considering* the possibility that there might, even *might*, exist a fossilized turtle with a fossilized celluloid collar button in its belly... well... this is not an institution with which I care to be affiliated.

At first old Dobbin did not seem to think that Uncle Jack fully understood the magnitude of the situation. He snorted and quivered and tugged at the bit. Uncle Jack made a sort of bridge or a roof out of himself by leaning over and putting his mouth close to Dobbin's ear. He told me to scrunch in between him and the horse, and I did.

I expect we were a sight, standing there in the middle of the muddy road without a bush or a barn for protection. Dobbin began to settle down. I don't know what Uncle Jack was whispering in his ear. Maybe he was explaining how much better it was to be caught in a red-hail storm than it was to get your hoof caught in the door of a Plymouth sedan. Whatever it was, it must have been better than "there, there," because old Dobbin did calm down.

It was Dobbin and Uncle Jack who took the brunt of that hail storm, and it must have been like taking a beating. When it finally passed over, going mostly east and north, Uncle Jack brought old Dobbin back to the real world by saying, "There, there," and brought me back to the real world by grinning and saying, "Son, that was a real piss-cutter!"

Lacking Uncle Jack's fluency in meteorological terminology, I accepted his opinion as gospel.

Later, when I told Aunt Tildy how we had nearly got drowned and hailed-on to death in a piss-cutter, she gave Uncle Jack a sour look. I realized then that she didn't know much more about weather words than I, but she was too proud to admit it.

We slogged our way on home, old Dobbin's hooves sucking up mud every step of the way.

After I had been nearly hugged to death by Aunt Tildy, stuffed with fried Rhode Island Red, and endured a moment of silence in respect for the Orpington who had been long ago pecked to death by the other hens, we sat on the front porch rocking and pondering.

"Red hail?" Aunt Tildy nearly ruined her health in laughter.

Uncle Jack let his pipe rest at ease on what little there was of his belly. "Red hail!" he assured her.

And red hail it was. Later I tried to tell them at the University about it. Unfortunately, they will never listen to anyone who does not have an advanced degree. And you never *get* an advanced degree if you try to discuss red hail.

23

All You Need to Know About the Hinges of Hell

The storm had hit Uncle Jack and Aunt Tildy's place, but not with the intensity which old Dobbin and Uncle Jack and I had endured on the mud road. There had been no hail, just some rain and a lot of wind.

We spent the first full day of my summer vacation replacing some of those rusty, flat tin cans which had blown off the Museum of the Battle of the Wilderness in the storm. Uncle Jack told me it was necessary to get this work done as soon as possible because the missing flat tin cans not only compromised the structural integrity of the building, but would soon be considered by the envious as a blot on the esthetic escutcheon of Comanche County.

I asked him if that would be worse than a piss-cutter, and he said it would be about the same. He told me that variations on what did and did not constitute esthetics in Comanche County required as much pondering and study as the Talmud.

Naturally I asked if Talmud was worse than the mud on the road east of Clearwater.

He did not answer me, but that was alright because I soon learned that his mind was on the change of seasons. That evening when we went inside, I heard him tell Aunt Tildy that it looked like it might be a long summer.

Well, I just hoped Uncle Jack was right. My summers in Comanche County always seemed too short to me.

Aunt Tildy took her broom and swept the little massasaugas off the rocking chairs and mostly off the porch. She did it gently because that was her way. She doubtless figured that rattlesnakes liked to be comfortable just like anybody else.

The wind had shifted around to the north, and there was just an eye-squint of sun left in the West. Uncle Jack twisted his rocker around so he could observe and admire the last rays bouncing and glittering off the new flat tin cans. He didn't mention how nice the Battle of the Wilderness Museum looked. He just smiled.

I was proud of our work. I reckoned that if anybody was going to have criticism ladled upon them for diluting the esthetics of Comanche County, it was dang sure not going to be Uncle Jack or me.

Aunt Tildy had just set down the pitcher of lemonade and begun the process of settling into her rocker when the telephone jangled long rings and short rings. Uncle Jack gave a lurch and slapped his hip for the Smith and Wesson he no longer carried regularly. Mostly he carried it when he wanted to welcome me or shoot a cloud in its roily under-belly.

"Gol-dang that thing!" he spluttered. "I rue the day!"

This statement did not exactly bowl me over like a bolt of lightning because Uncle Jack "rued the day" every time the phone rang.

My family did not accept scientific advancement grace-fully. Only around 1939 did my father reluctantly declare that the ice cube tray was, maybe and perhaps, the greatest human achievement since sap became syrup.

Yet Uncle Jack, for the most part, admired progress. The steam engine was "just elegant" to Uncle Jack. He read such of the latest magazines as he could get his hands on, and even though he had never owned one, could explain the workings of the internal combustion engine until your eyes drooped.

The problem Uncle Jack had with the telephone was the leap of faith required to believe that the human voice could be scrunched down and pushed through a copper wire. "It can not work, and it will never work," Uncle Jack said. The fact that it *did* work in no way ruffled Uncle Jack's scientif-ic feathers.

We sat there, Uncle Jack and I, while Aunt Tildy per-formed the minor heresy of pretending to talk to someone maybe a mile away.

I poured a lemonade for Uncle Jack and one for myself. He filled and lit his briar pipe and seemed to find a balm in it, easing the indignity of having to live in the same world as the telephone.

By the time Aunt Tildy came back out, Uncle Jack was balmed to the point of snorey unconsciousness, and his briar pipe, left to fend for itself, rested at a dangerous angle on his lap.

We talked quietly so as not to disturb Uncle Jack. I still had lots I wanted to tell her about how we had survived the piss-cutter. But something told me I, maybe, had already said too much.

Suddenly Uncle Jack came up out of that old rocking chair roaring almost as loud as a piss-cutter. His overalls were asmolder.

Immediately Aunt Tildy, with a presence of mind which made me proud to know her, picked up the pitcher of lemonade and poured it down the front of Uncle Jack's pants.

That act was not as easy as it sounds because after roaring out of the rocker, Uncle Jack's first reaction was to severely wallop the afflicted area in an effort to beat out the smolder.

I am of the opinion that if Uncle Jack had been given the time to consider this course of action, he probably would not have chosen it. And I am sure Aunt Tildy would not have recommended it because it is difficult to pour lemonade down the front of a mans pants when he is doubled up in the worst kind of agony.

When Uncle Jack finally sat back down, he was soaked in indignation and embarrassment and lemonade. He held his hairy hand over the lately endangered area, and I expect it would have required a significant number of piss-cutters to pull his hand away.

"Is there any more lemonade, Tildy?"

"Lemonade? Lemonade! Jack Freeman, I submit that you have had your allotted portion of lemonade and mine and young Max's as well."

Uncle Jack pondered this and took it in good grace.

"You did right, Tildy, and I thank you. That was hot as the hinges of Hell."

Aunt Tildy pondered a while on that with growing agitation. Finally she stamped her bony little feet on the porch floor and said, "Wait a minute. Starting on our wedding night and numerous times thereafter you have brought up the subject of 'hotter than the hinges of Hell.' I freely admit that I am not a well-educated person, but it occurs to me that any future life I may have will be meaningless and, perhaps, squandered unless I know, precisely, the temperature of the hinges of Hell."

Not for the first time I realized that Aunt Tildy was wise.

Once Uncle Jack told me Aunt Tildy was more wise than the seven wise virgins. I pondered that and asked him if there had also been seven dumb virgins. He told me, "Yes, but not for very long."

Anyway, Aunt Tildy was wise enough to know that such a challenge as she had just cast would take his mind off his aggrieved areas.

"Hell," Uncle Jack did not hesitate to tell us, "maintains a yearly average of 590 degrees; and that is only on the first level. As to the hinges, the ones on the outer-most gate would burn a blister on a petrified porcupine. And the further down you go, the hotter it gets. In late July and on through August, 612 degrees would be considered balmy. But the fiendish thing about Hell is that every two and a half hours the Devil makes you run around in a room full of ice, which chills you so much you are soon banging on the door to get back into the oven. And so the sufferers and the suffragettes glare at old Satan and say, 'This is just pure Hell!' And old Satan grins back and says, 'Yulp, I am humbly proud.'

"Now, the Hell for Baptists usually runs twelve to eighteen degrees hotter and is in a special annex which is off to the left as you go in. The extra heat is not because the Devil has it in for the Baptists especially, but because the Baptists feel they deserve a little extra."

"Now," Aunt Tildy observed, "it has been my understanding since childhood that Hell has lots of different little nooks and crannies and at least three floors reserved for various sins and various degrees of dumbness."

I could see Uncle Jack's umbrage growing ridged, and that was because he understood Aunt Tildy was narrowing in for a sharp jab at anyone dumb enough to expose his trousers to a briar pipe conflagration.

Uncle Jack cleared his throat to give himself time to clear his mind. He eyed the empty lemonade pitcher, and I expect he would have given four acres of bottom land for a cool sip. But the lemonade had been sacrificed in a far more noble cause.

"As to the nooks and crannies of Hell, and whether it has floors reserved for the various sins and dumbness of mankind," he said, "I can not answer with any degree of certitude. But the next time I am in Coldwater I will inquire."

Aunt Tildy's little bird-eyes sparkled. "Old man," she told him, "with the kind of life you have led I expect that someday *you* will be the foremost authority on the nooks and crannies of Hell."

I guess Uncle Jack had at least found some of the nooks and crannies of "uncomfortableness." He stood and mustered as much dignity as one might reasonably be expected to muster when he wears singed and lemonade-wet trousers.

"My body shall," he explained in a tone which absolutely precluded doubt, "when my time comes, rest comfortably in my sarcophagus while my soul wings its way to Heaven where it shall, through all eternity, sit at the right hand of Jenny Lind, the Swedish Nightingale."

I wanted to ask who Jenny Lind was, but Uncle Jack had proudly stepped into the house and Aunt Tildy was doubled over shrieking with laughter and hollering "Bull hocky!"

As with so many of the stories I heard on that front porch, this one whetted my young appetite. Goodness, I was a sponge soaking up history! Years later at the university, I wrote a paper entitled "Considerations on the Soul of Jenny Lind and its Relevance to Comanche County, Kansas." The paper was never published, but I had the feeling more of the faculty recognized me later as I walked by.

24

Uncle Jack and the Great Range War

The Great Range War happened years before I was born, and I learned the complete and accurate account of it from at least some of those involved. After I submitted my research paper "Concerning the Great Range War of Comanche County" to my professor, he returned it to me with more red lines on it than a street map of Kansas City.

"I can find no reference to a Range War in Comanche County and no reference to anyone named Leepy Danfer." The professor told me, "Can you prove his existence?"

I braced him up against the wall after class and asked if he could prove the existence of Cleopatra or Patrick Henry. He told me I was being ridiculous and that I should please not stand so close. He told me Cleopatra and Patrick Henry were well-established in history, but that, anyway, they were dead." He could not show me proof that they had existed.

I suppose I, perhaps, persuaded him to be closer to the wall than he had intended to become upon arising that morning. I could smell the spearmint on his breath. I told him, "Old son, there are damn few people who have more compelling qualifications in the realm of being dead than Leepy Danfer."

Leepy Danfer had bought the spread next to Uncle Jack and Aunt Tildy. He was dead and amoldering in his grave long before I heard about him. According to Aunt Tildy, he was dead because he had been a cattle-rustling scalawag and according to Uncle Jack, he was dead because he had been a son-of-a-bitch.

That is mostly the way it was told, except that sometimes it was Aunt Tildy who said he had been a son-of-a-bitch and Uncle Jack who said he had been a scalawag.

However, by and large and for the most part, he was dead because Uncle Jack shot him through the heart using a .45 caliber Smith and Wesson cartridge, which is a little shorter than the .45 caliber Colt variety (which will not fit into the cylinder of a Smith and Wesson, although the Smith and Wesson will fit into the Colt). It runs in my mind that the .45 Smith and Wesson cartridge was about three-sixteenths of an inch shorter than that of the Colt.

I doubt if Leepy Danfer noticed the difference.

Leepy Danfer lies buried beneath a scraggly cedar tree on what had been his own property until the court granted the property to Uncle Jack because Leepy Danfer had siphoned off so many of Uncle Jack's cattle that even a judge who was a Democrat had to admit that it was only right and proper.

I have always considered it a shining example of Uncle Jack's generosity that within two weeks of the court's decision he deeded exactly half of that land over to the Judge. Uncle Jack was even more than generous because he gave the Judge the half which contained the scraggly cedar tree and the molding remains of Leepy Danfer.

Uncle Jack told me that he and the Judge had conferred at length on the possibility of erecting a marker for Leepy. The problem was they could not agree on whether the stone should read "Scalawag" or "Son-of-a-bitch," and in the end, as so often happens, nothing got done.

As I understand it, when old Leepy moved in, Uncle Jack and Aunt Tildy drove over in the buckboard to get acquainted. They carried a welcoming gift of homemade biscuits in the pan in which they were baked. Mr. Leepy Danfer accepted the gift without much emotion. Although the pan was warmly and good-smellingly presented, old Leepy never returned it. In as much as that pan was Aunt Tildy's favorite baking pan, it seemed comfortable and appropriate for her to call him a son-of-a-bitch on occasion.

Now that I think about it, it *was* mostly Aunt Tildy who called Leepy a son-of-a-bitch and Uncle Jack who called him a scalawag.

Uncle Jack and Aunt Tildy did not attend the funeral because it would have been unseemly. Besides, after having just shot Leepy Danfer through the heart, Uncle Jack indicated a more or less sudden and intense interest in viewing the flora and the fauna often found in the remote hills of Oklahoma.

Aunt Tildy prepared and sent a dish of green beans for

the lunch after the funeral, but she did not put any bacon in them. Maybe God could forgive Leepy Danfer for being a cattle rustler and a scalawag, but God had not lost his favorite baking pan.

That Uncle Jack's cattle operation had prospered at all was mostly a matter of luck. The management of a major Civil War museum, the polishing of a Battle of the Wilderness right-brogan and a Battle of the Wilderness bugle understandably did not leave him an abundance of leisure time. Eventually, however, even Uncle Jack had to face up to the fact that his cattle were disappearing, hoof over horn.

Although the details are lost in the mist of time, who should appear one day silhouetted against the horizon other than Uncle Jack? And who should he find stealing his cattle other than Leepy Danfer? And so he shot Leepy through the heart with a .45 Smith and Wesson cartridge, or rather, the lead slug there-from. I already mentioned that I doubt it made much difference to Leepy Danfer if the Smith and Wesson cartridge was (and I wish I could remember exactly) about 3/16 of an inch shorter than the Colt.

After the shooting, Uncle Jack wheeled into the yard and found Aunt Tildy in back making soap, which is what she mostly did, even though she already had enough bricks of soap laid up to adequately supply a dormitory for a complete drum and bugle corps and the alto section of the Coldwater Methodist Church. (Now, this is in no manner intended as a criticism of the alto section, although Mrs. Allager, who was the choir director, did seem to lean heavily toward altos.)

"I have just shot Leepy Danfer through the heart, and I have a sudden and intense interest in viewing the flora and the fauna of the remote hills of Oklahoma," Uncle Jack announced.

Aunt Tildy asked him had he thought to retrieve her favorite baking pan. He said, "No."

Like so many things, her reply is lost in the mists of time.

But I know this: Uncle Jack went south with his saddle bags chuck full of bacon, and afterwards, anyone at the funeral lunch in honor of Mr. Leepy Danfer who might reasonably be expecting bacon in his green beans was doomed to disappointment.

No relatives stepped foreword to claim the remains of Leepy Danfer, and the folks who seemed to run Comanche County were not outlandishly enthusiastic about absorbing the cost of burying someone who was at best, a scalawag and in all probability, a son-of-a-bitch. That is the reason Leepy Danfer was buried beneath a scraggly cedar tree, with no bacon in the green beans for his afterwards luncheon.

Aunt Tildy said it was about eleven days later—actually, the night of the eleventh day—when Uncle Jack rode in under the cover of the dark of the moon.

It was Aunt Tildy's conviction that Uncle Jack would have preferred to sneak in by way of the back porch, but in as much as he had not yet gotten around to building a back porch, that was not feasible.

I have no reason to believe that their reunion was anything less than joyous because I have never witnessed two people who seemed to have such a need for each other. Aunt Tildy told me that Uncle Jack was a little miffed at first because she had not built a back porch in anticipation of his dark-of-the-moon return. He said, "Dag nab it, Tildy, when a fellow shoots another fellow it seems to me like the least his wife could do would be build a back porch!"

Aunt Tildy, seeking to dull down the edge of Uncle Jack's ire, apologized for neglecting her wifely duty. Uncle Jack softened his tone by allowing that it need not be a very large porch.

There was no great stir or hubbub caused by Uncle Jack's shooting of Leepy Danfer. Eventually, the Sheriff rode out and expressed an interest that Uncle Jack curb his inclination to shoot people. Uncle Jack told him that he had been thinking along the same lines and that he was trying to break the habit.

As the sheriff started back down the lane, Aunt Tildy hollered an inquiry as to the probabilities of the restoration of a favorite baking pan to its rightful owner. Just because the scalawag was dead did not, in her opinion, give him perpetual rights to an object which was meant to convey such biscuits as were intended to be gifts. But where the hell did he get the idea he could keep the pan?

"Come back here, you scalawag," she hollered at the sheriff. "If this is the land of the free and the home of the brave, then where is my baking pan?"

Well, sir, that old Sheriff turned his horse around and touched his fingers to the brim of his hat. "I thank you kindly, Ma'am," he told her. "I have been trying to decide if I should run for another term, and you have just made up my mind."

25

Captain Jack O'Hare Earns a Demerit

My greatest disappointment as I performed the sad task of sorting through Uncle Jack and Aunt Tildy's effects was finding that neither of them had kept a diary. How I should like to have a more exact time frame in which to pigeon-hole the tales which lay with no semblance of chronological order in my mind! For my part, in those times when I was present when something happened, I was often too young for a particular year to have meaning for me. Sharp images remain in my mind of how things sounded, looked and even smelled at a given time. But as for specific dates of happenings through those Comanche County summers…they roil and overlap like summer clouds.

Emmot Pierce God-damned his mule up the lane towards the porch where Aunt Tildy rocked and worried. It was long before I came on the scene. Captain Jack O'Hare was a very sick bunny.

It is not my wish to offend, but you had just as well get used to the idea that if one is going to write about mules one must use "God damn" and similarly distasteful words. Furthermore, if you are to gain knowledge of Comanche County, I would be remiss if I failed to report that that was the phrase Emmot Pierce used to encourage his mule up the lane towards the porch.

I will also tell you that as I worked toward my degree in history, I became interested in writing for the University newspaper. My first article began in this manner: "Emmot Pierce G'damned his mule up the lane..."

I was soundly admonished for even thinking about using such language in the University newspaper and told that the adjacent Bible College would, in all probability, consider me the Anti-Christ. I already knew that.

The Bible College had some slippery connection with the University, and to tell you the truth, the Bible College had been my first choice in regard to higher learning. Thanks to Uncle Jack, I was as well grounded in the Bible as I was in the history of Kansas.

I was ushered into a fine, walnut-walled room, where a spavined-looking old lady wearing a sparkly American-flag pin on her breast looked me up and down. She did not seem to see in me much hope for the future of Christianity.

Almost before I settled in on the straight-backed oak chair, she commenced on me. "Recite the first Bible verse which comes into your mind!" she demanded.

I shot right back at her: "And the beast shall be of four

legs and upon his back shall he convey a handsome warrior
and a kid with a brown cardboard suitcase. And his name
shall be called Dobbin and Dobbin shall be his name.
Pharisees 1:11."

"Jesus Christ," she almost whistled.

"No, Ma'am," I corrected, "Pharisees 1:11."

She next explained to me that I was the Anti-Christ and
used other words which are, curiously enough, usually
mostly used when addressing mules.

And that is how I did not enter the Bible College but
entered the University as a history major. I was then kicked
off the University newspaper because I had rightfully mentioned that Emmot Pierce had G'damned his mule.

It has been my observation that most college professors
are bicycle-riders or Studebaker drivers and frankly do just
not know one great hell of a lot about mules.

As a general rule, I would say the average college professor can rant for three hours concerning the Isosceles tri-
angle or the Pythagorean theory without ever saying
"G'damn." But put him on a mule going up a muddy lane,
and I expect he would learn pretty fast—except for history
professors.

I was quite young when I first heard the following story,
but I remember it very well. Years later, when I thought I
was grown, Aunt Tildy remembered it better to me.

"Emmot Pierce was about as near to being a veterinari-
an as anyone we had for miles around," Aunt Tildy said,
"but he was lazy and cantankerous and it nearly took an act
of God to get him to do any work. With Captain Jack
O'Hare lying sick and perhaps dying, your Uncle was not
about to wait for God. 'Hell, for all I know God might be in
Indiana or McCook, Nebraska,' is what he told me. So Jack

strapped on his Smith and Wesson, saddled old Dobbin, and rode out to fetch Emmot Pierce.

"Now, remember what I told you?" she asked me, "Emmot Pierce sat his mule in a peculiar fashion. He rode without saddle, sitting on the most hindermost part of the mule as could be considered feasible, his ankles crossed Indian-style in front of him on the mule's back.

"So Emmot Pierce G'damned his mule up to the front porch with Jack, astride old Dobbin, right behind him. Jack had his hand on his Smith and Wesson and was looking ominous as a basket of snake eggs.

Emmot Pierce sat there on that mule, a pot-gutted specimen of a man with long, sharpish yellow teeth which would have jealoused an alligator. Emmot took his time, most likely trying to act calmer than he felt, and from mule-height tipped his hat. 'Afternoon, Tildy,' he said.

"Your Uncle Jack seemed not to be in the mood for social discourse. He made a throat-sound which I had not previously known to be in his repertoire, but I guess Emmot Pierce did because he unscrewed his bony legs pretty fast and slipped off that mule. With his little leather satchel he followed Jack over to where the Captain lay writhing in pitiful misery.

"Now, I will say this for old Emmot Pierce. He didn't try to rush the job. I suppose he figured himself for a dead man if he had tried. But he touched lightly and prodded softly and said 'Hmm,' and 'Tisk-Tisk.' He looked in the Captain's eyes and examined his throat while all the time he was saying, 'There, there, good bunny.' Finally, without it being noticed, he had worked his way between the Captain and Uncle Jack. He made a quick duck of his head and a quick movement with his hands. I saw Jack's hand slide toward his Smith and Wesson, but before he could draw his weapon, Emmot Pierce flashed him a big yellow-toothed grin and said, 'He'll be fine.'

"Emmot Pierce took Jack by the arm and led him several steps away and whispered something in his ear which caused your Uncle to let out a loud cowboy-*whoop* and declare that he would be pure and simple gol-danged.

"Then, Emmot Pierce, with more cash in his pocket than he could have ever thought possible, handed Jack a little can of salve from the leather satchel and started happily toward home perched atop his mule.

"'What in the world is it, Jack?' I asked.

"Jack gave me a stern look and said, 'I am afraid the young Captain has earned his first demerit.'"

As Aunt Tildy and I laughed and reminisced, it occurred to me that I had never really understood just what Captain Jack O'Hare's problem had been those many years ago. Aunt Tildy cackled and spilled some of her lemonade. "You didn't know? Why he had a dose of the clap! Yes, sir, cute little bunny-clap."

I could scarcely wait for my classes at the University to resume that fall! After settling in, I went immediately to the library and found the section which contained the books on veterinary science. After I had spent two days asking for book after book, the librarian finally asked if she could be of help. I explained I was researching for a paper to be called "Concerning Venereal Disease Among Jackrabbits in Comanche County."

Well, I expect that lady would not have jumped backwards any faster had she seen a massasauga. "WHAT?" she asked, in a pitch I would judge to be D sharp.

"You know," I told her, "bunny-clap."

If had I found my place in academia, I would never have called a student a "pervert" nor a "monster." Once again I found myself profoundly perplexed at the obstacles placed in my way on my journey toward a higher education.

26

The Strange Ordeal of
Thunder Johnson

I have no doubt that behind my back people call me "Windy." They do not call me "Windy" to my face because it has become my habit to wear Uncle Jack's smooth old Smith and Wesson. The cartridges for the .45 caliber Smith and Wesson are a little shorter than that of the .45 Colt, but the gun does seem to discourage people from calling me "Windy" to my face.

Having dredged up the memory of old Emmot Pierce and his mule, I'll say it's funny the way one memory brings on another. As far as I know, about the only thing Emmot Pierce and Thunder Johnson had in common was that they both lived close to Uncle Jack and Aunt Tildy's place.

"Close," of course, is a relative term and does not mean the same in Comanche County as it would, for instance, in New York City or Emporia, Kansas.

Thunder Johnson was a familiar sight to me. He lived about a mile east and a quarter mile south, and I couldn't count the times I watched him ride by. Sometimes he turned up our lane for a visit, and sometimes he didn't. He rode a rangy old piebald named Lucky, and it was Thunder Johnson astride Lucky whom Uncle Jack and I met once on our way home from Coldwater in the buckboard.

In those days it would have been unthinkable for neighbors to meet on the road and not pull up to say "howdy." Old Thunder Johnson doffed his wide-rimmed straw hat and wiped his brow with his sleeve. "Jack," he said, "I've been wanting to see you about buying a young heifer."

"Hell," Uncle Jack told him, "why don't you just *steal* one like everybody else?" That suggestion fell a little short of humor because, like almost everyone in Comanche County, Thunder Johnson remembered Leepy Danfer and how he lay amoldering in his grave. And, though I didn't know it until that evening, Thunder Johnson had come close to meeting his maker once before, and was, therefore, more than willing to pay whatever money was required for his heifer, so as to avoid a recurrence.

When supper was over and the chores finished, Uncle Jack made a trip to his trunk upstairs. Aunt Tildy and I took our places on the front porch and settled in for the evening. By and by Uncle Jack came out grinning and handed me an undated article torn from *The Coldwater Talisman:*

> It is with regret that we learn of the hitting of, by lightning, of one of our neighbors to the east, Mr. Thurman Johnson. Neighbors

report that Mr. Johnson (according to Mrs. Johnson) was sitting in a reclining position beneath one of their best peach trees when a small but treacherous cloud passed overhead, suddenly dispatching a bolt of lightning which did not really hurt the tree but ripened all of the peaches on the west side into "a sort of sparkly sweetness." *The Talisman* has it on reliable authority that the cobbler made therefrom was one of the finest cobblers Mrs. Johnson has ever made. She bemoans not being able to make lightning happen to peach trees when she needs it, because she believes, if she could, she would certainly win first prize at the fair.

Beneath that, and mostly torn off, was an intriguing item about a local citizen who had made an emergency trip to Council Grove because his eldest sister had caught appendicitis and was not expected to live. I don't know if she did or not, because most of the article was torn off.

According to Uncle Jack, Mr. Thurman Johnson was called "Thunder" because he had been hit by lightning. And the reason his piebald horse was called "Lucky" was because half way through the gelding process, Mr. Johnson was overcome with an overpowering desire to sit in a reclining position beneath a peach tree. So Mr. Johnson applied a healing balm to the offended part of the horse, which had been very offended indeed, and hied himself unto the orchard.

Uncle Jack told me it was his opinion that Lucky was likely confused in his feelings in regard to Thunder Johnson, although Thunder was still called Thurman because he had not yet been struck by lightning and his wife had not yet made a peach cobbler which could be regarded in any way as exceptional.

Uncle Jack rocked and pondered on how a horse might reasonably be expected to feel about being half-way gelded. Without question it would be fifty percent better than being one hundred percent gelded, but by the same token, it would also be one hundred percent better had he (the horse) not shown up for work that day.

In any case, Uncle Jack explained that old Lucky apparently eventually reached the conclusion that half a loaf was better than none, and so he forgave Thunder Johnson his trespass or his one-half trespass.

The tapping out of the dottle from Uncle Jack's pipe and the tamping in of fresh tobacco gave Aunt Tildy time to avail herself of a ponder.

"How," she eventually wondered outloud, "do *loaves* fit into a story about a one-half gelded horse, a peach tree, and a lightning-enhanced cobbler? I will tell you straight out, Jack Freeman, if this turns into a parable, and if any fishes or multitudes on mountains appear, I will not stand for it!"

"Now, Tildy…"

"Don't 'now Tildy,' me!" She told him. "It has been my observation that 67% of your stories eventually get mixed all up with loaves, fishes or multitudes, and tonight I am not in the frame of mind to listen to anything remotely resembling a dad-gummed multitude."

"How about attitudes or altitudes or Beatitudes?"

"No, sir, "tudes" give me the hives, and unless you enjoy having me scratch all night, leave them out." Aunt Tildy tried a tentative scratch.

"Well, now, what exactly is your position concerning

fishes?" Uncle Jack asked.

"Fishes, as a general rule, don't give me hives, but given the choice between, say, a story with fishes and a story with grasshoppers, I would choose the grasshoppers."

"In all honesty, Tildy, it is extremely difficult to work either fishes *or* grasshoppers into a story about a half-gelded horse."

Uncle Jack held another kitchen match to his pipe and sucked in the pleasure. "I remember that year especially well because of the grasshoppers," he began. Aunt Tildy winked at me from behind her palmetto fan.

"But now that I think of it, maybe it was the *next* year the grasshoppers got so bad. Oh, we had plenty of grasshoppers the year I'm telling about, but in no way shape nor form could they be described as a 'multitude.'"

He paused, and then—so fast his words almost ran together—he said, "Yes, it was the next year when they came in multitudes and started eating all the loaves and…"

Aunt Tildy uncoiled from her rocking chair and stamped her little birdie-feet down hard. "Now, stop that!"

"I expect it was around early June when Thunder decided to put old Lucky with a mare. Myself, I wasn't sure if that were a kindness or a cruelness, and I guess old Lucky wasn't sure either. It seemed to put him in a sort of quandary; about fifty percent of the time he seemed interested, and the other fifty percent of the time he ignored the mare completely. Whether his ambivalence was due to lack of knowledge, lack of desire, or lack of confidence, we will never know. But I figure if ever any horse needed the ability to scratch his head and ponder what to do next, it was old Lucky."

Uncle Jack settled into silence as if the story was over.

I knew it was not; he was just waiting for me to ask the question, so I did: "Well, what happened?"

"Well, what happened was this: every day old Thunder got fidgetier and fidgetier concerning if he was ever to get a colt out of old Lucky. And finally, in desperation, he poured half a bottle of *Comanche County Confidence* down old Lucky's throat. Well, now, after that the horse roared around the pasture as fast as a Battle of the Wilderness cannon ball. It was a plain and simple case of *Ad Astra Per Aspera*. It was also a case of over-compensation, because in a few months that mare dropped the finest set of twin colts I ever saw.

"Now, Mrs. Thunder Johnson won the peach pie competition at the county fair for the next three years running. And that was because she had canned all of the peaches which had been ripened by lightning. In the ecstasy of getting twin colts, old Thunder betook himself and a bottle of *Comanche County Celebration* and sat, yet again, in a reclining position beneath that same peach tree. And that was where the lightning came and found him a second time—and this time, it killed him deader than Kelsey's nuts."

"Bull hocky, Uncle Jack," I told him. "We just saw him today on the road back from Coldwater."

Uncle Jack pulled his thumb and forefinger down his long nose and looked at me sadly. "Son, I didn't want to tell you just before you crawled away into your dark and lonely bed, but that was not Thunder Johnson we met today. Thunder Johnson lies amoldering in his dark and lonely grave. What we saw was what is called an 'apparition.' Apparitions are about the same as ghosts but 7% meaner."

"Bull hocky!" Aunt Tildy told him quietly, and that was

when Uncle Jack made a lunge for her and cried, "MULTI-TUDES!"

Aunt Tildy nearly jumped out of her skin.

27

Uncle Jack Gets His Sarcophagus

Regrettable as it is that I found no diaries in what Uncle Jack and Aunt Tildy left behind, I did find several albums of snapshots. I believe Aunt Tildy must have had one of the first Kodaks in Comanche County, and what fun they had with it! They are all there, Aunt Tildy squinting into the sun holding an old rooster whose neck she has just wrung, Uncle Jack in his G.A.R. uniform with his sword with the ivory hilt, and Captain Jack O'Hare, with his cantilevered-spring-loaded-articulated prosthesis. There was Art, the son who died too young. He died before I was born, leaving a gap in the family for me to fill, unknowingly, years later. There was little Lucy who lived to a mature age, and died having the time of her life. There was Charlie who, to Uncle Jack's mortification, established the first marshmallow delivery route in Kansas and died a fat but wealthy man. And there was Ben, whose death by whiffletree was unusual, even for Comanche County.

I sat back on the floor when I found those snapshots, sat for half a day wishing for them their original sharpness and contrast—wishing away the ghosty-whiteness encroaching from the edges. I make no apology for my tears nor my laughter.

My soul and body! There was at least half an album containing photo documentation of what became known as "Freeman's Folly," Uncle Jack's sarcophagus. Make no mistake about it, Uncle Jack got his sarcophagus.

How many evenings we spent on the front porch reliving the story of the sarcophagus I have no idea, but I know that story by heart.

Dutch Henkensiepen was a stone mason and stone carver up in Pratt County. Uncle Jack heard about him when he was in Coldwater buying a new, light, trim little one-seat buggy. Aunt Tildly described the buggy as "Cute as a bug's ear," with a fold-down top and an isinglass window in the back. It had little kerosene lamps on the sides, all black and brass, with colored marbles in the sides and rear. "I could have just sat up all night admiring those little jewel marbles," she admitted.

I judge that the first photo of the "Sarcophagus" series must have been taken by Art. It shows Uncle Jack and Aunt Tildy both dressed fit to kill, sitting in the buggy with Dobbin hitched and eager.

It had been Aunt Tildy's contention when she heard about Dutch Henkensiepen that Uncle Jack should simply write and inquire if he might be interested in hollowing out a sarcophagus rock. But Uncle Jack took umbrage and told her that from what he had heard, the average sarcophagus carver could not fit a sarcophagus lid "for sour-green owl stuff," and it was not his desire to spend eternity with a slow drizzle of cold water dripping on his face.

Aunt Tildy admitted that, what with making soap and keeping the family going, she had likely fallen woefully behind in sarcophagul advancements and so she would defer to his judgment.

So on a hot, dusty July day, Art snapped the shutter on the Kodak, Uncle Jack did his tongue-click to old Dobbin, and he and Aunt Tildy were off for Pratt County. Aunt Tildy had packed a fried chicken lunch, and along about noon they found a shady place beside a creek and broke out the picnic basket. Uncle Jack snapped a picture of Aunt Tildy holding a drumstick to her mouth, and Aunt Tildy took a picture of Uncle Jack holding a drumstick to his mouth. His eyes are crinkled in mirth and happiness as if shopping for a sarcophagus was about the most pleasant pursuit to which a fellow might aspire. As strange as it may seem, Aunt Tildy was all for Uncle Jack buying a sarcophagus. I guess a lot of women would have moaned and wailed, facing up to the fact that their husbands were mortal. However, I'm not sure Aunt Tildy really believed Uncle Jack was mortal.

As Uncle Jack told it, by mid-afternoon Aunt Tildy was kind of wilted down and looking peaked. They were into Pratt County but still had to go almost to the northern border. Well, Uncle Jack made a few inquires of folks they met along the road, and by and by, they found themselves at what passed for a small boarding house.

"It was run by a handsome Christian widow named Mrs.

Judson," Uncle Jack announced. "She had massive thighs, and her skin was the color of pure cream."

Aunt Tildy indulged herself with a loud guffaw. "The only thing 'pure' about this story is that it's pure bull hocky! What the widow Judson had was a massive nose and a massive goiter."

Uncle Jack filled his pipe with deliberation, then somewhat weakly, somewhat feebly, announced that he had always found women with goiters particularly attractive. "It's one more thing to love," he said.

"Max," Aunt Tildy told me, "Go in to the telephone and call the *In*sane Asylum. Tell them to bring a net and a strong rope. I always knew that sooner or later it would come to this."

Uncle Jack addressed the porch ceiling and said, "Father, if it be Thy will, let this cup of noses and goiters pass from me."

Aunt Tildy, putting more faith in negotiations than in prayer said, "Look, if you will concede the massive goiter, I am willing to admit the possibility of *one* massive thigh, and we will forget the massive nose."

It seemed like a fair trade to me, but Uncle Jack had a sort of perplexed look.

Finally he seemed to find the root of his problem. "It appears to me that if she only has *one* massive thigh she will be presented as off-balance and grotesque—which is unfair and contrary to fact."

"Gol-dang it," Aunt Tildy declared, "Just leave it to a man to complicate the most simple procedure. Put the gol-dang goiter on one side and the gol-dang massive thigh on the other and get on with the story!"

There was a short space of near silence, disturbed only

by the creaking of rocking chairs and the singing of cicadas.

"The first impression one might get in seeing the Widow Judson," Uncle Jack began, choosing his words carefully and thoughtfully, "was that of a well-balanced woman. If she had any unusual physical characteristics at all they were well hidden beneath an outlandishly large collar and a billowy long skirt."

"Nondescript," Aunt Tildy suggested.

"Handsomely nondescript," Uncle Jack amended, and Aunt Tildy let it go.

"Well-read and well-spoken," Uncle Jack ventured.

"Get to the part about the tallywhackers," Aunt Tildy told him.

"The tallywhackers are a way down the road. First, there is the mule. Now, the indisputable reason her husband died is because of chronic mule-kick, and chronic mule-kick is the worst kind of kick. It must be differentiated from acute mule-kick because in acute mule-kick, the mule only kicks you a time or two. It may be serious and it may be painful and it may be fatal, but, all in all, it's just normal mule behavior. With chronic mule-kick, the kicker gives the kickee a couple of the acute variety and finds it so pleasant and invigorating that it continues kicking until the kickee looks like what comes out of the exhaust end of a pulp mill. But, howsome-ever, the event was woefully unpleasant for the widow Judson and likely even more unpleasant for the late, and sadly lamented Mr. Judson. The chronic mule kick brought about the acquaintance of widow Judson and Mr. Dutch Henkensiepen.

"It is my opinion," Uncle Jack continued, "that a normal coffin would have accommodated the remains of three or four chronic mule-kicked-men, but there being only one mule-kicked-man available at the time, the widow Judson determined to do what was right, even if it was an unconscionable waste of space."

"Lordy, Lordy, Lordy," Aunt Tildy told him. "With the possible exception of those cucumber sandwich-eating professors at Emporia Normal School, nobody gives a rat's patooti about wasted coffin space. Tell about the tally-whackers."

"Now, Tildy, the cucumber sandwiches are, as yet, an unsubstantiated rumor, though I believe it is probably true. The tallywhackers are still a way down the road. First must come the funeral and the gnashing of teeth and the burial and the period of mourning. First must come the deep remorse for things done and things not done, for words said and the words not said."

"And the words I say are: *gol-dang* the funeral and the teeth and the black weeds of mourning!" Aunt Tildy's patience was wearing thin.

It still stands in my mind as a monument to his love for Aunt Tildy that Uncle Jack could bring himself to forgo a complete description of the funeral, the long, sad procession to the burial ground, and the afterwards-luncheon.

Uncle Jack rocked and pondered. "Well, sir, as the days and weeks passed and the balm of Gilead soothed the widow's soul and softened the memories of the funeral and the gnashing of teeth, she fell to considering what might be an appropriate marker for the Mister's final resting place. And that brought her to the doorstep of Mr. Dutch Henkensiepen."

"And the tallywhackers." Aunt Tildy put in, with only a trace of triumph in her voice.

"And the tallywhackers," Uncle Jack allowed.

"Although the widow Judson would have rather died a thousand slow and painful deaths than have that word pass her lovely, sensual lips."

Aunt Tildy's response was predictable and rapid. "Bull hocky," She told him. "Her lips were nearly hidden by her massive nose!"

"The *male appendage*." Uncle Jack declared, "That was the widow's term. And it was her opinion that the male appendage was what brought Mr. Dutch Henkensiepen to the low station in life in which she found him. She told your Aunt and me that he was a true artist and a stickler for accuracy. When he carved cherubim and seraphim on a gravestone, there was no doubt as to which were the girl cherubim and seraphim and which were the boy cherubim and seraphim.

"Understandably, in my opinion, the fair sex objected to having their final resting places adorned and perhaps fixed in the memories of countless generations by male appendages—not withstanding that they were on cherubim or seraphim. The dilemma lay in the fact that Dutch Henkensiepen was the only stone carver in at least a hundred miles, and he refused to compromise his artistic integrity. But the widow Judson told us with a charming blush that good old Kansas ingenuity had triumphed.

"After Mr. Henkensiepen had set a stone and packed up his tools and gone home, the bereaved family would quietly appear with a hammer. When they left, the boy and the girl seraphim and cherubim looked very much the same.

"The widow said over time it became a habit with the stone mason to return to the cemetery and pick up the little things. When she visited him, Dutch Henkensiepen had a nail keg half-full of male appendages.

"But the desecration of his art took a fearsome toll on the man. The Widow Judson declared it was a sorrowful sight watching a sober and industrious man take to the bottle.

"And that's how we found him," Uncle Jack concluded. "With his nose in a bottle."

"Drunk as a hoot owl!" Aunt Tildy agreed, "But solid-built and a fine specimen of a man, with massive thighs."

"Bull hocky!" Uncle Jack told her. "He had legs like a shikepoke and a purple wen on the top of his head.

"...But, be that as it may, he was the first man I had found who knew a 'sarcophagus' from an 'esophagus,' and he sobered up and brightened up immediately. That he was somewhat dubious and skeptical was understandable.

"'You want this sarcophagus with or without cherubim and seraphim?'

"With," I told him. "As many as you can cram on it."

"He took that favorably but cautiously. 'You want these cherubim and seraphim—ah—with or without?'

"Well, before I could get a word in, your Aunt Tildy told him, 'If I can't tell the boys from the girls at fifty feet, we won't pay you a rat's patooti for it!'

"I am fully convinced that, had Tildy desired a slave for life, she had just found one in Dutch Henkensiepen.

"He started telling us about a quarry up somewhere around Junction City where he could get fine, white lime-stone—solid chunks for the sarcophagus and the lid. Then, to get my measurement, he stood me up against a shed, and with a chisel, marked my height on the side of it.

"It's not hard to order a sarcophagus when you find the right man.

"The plan was, he would have the two stones shipped to

him by rail, one for the sarcophagus itself and one for the lid. When the job was finished, he would haul it down here in his big old wagon. So we finished up the details and the terms and started for home.

"All the way down Mr. Henkensiepen's lane, your Aunt Tildy shouted back at him: 'At fifty feet! The boys from the girls! Or you don't get so much as a rat's patooti!'

"Old Dutch hollered back, part in English and part in German. As near as I could tell, he was saying he would rather eat human flesh than disappoint her in the area of appendages."

In Uncle Jack's trunk I found postcards sent periodically and randomly from the Pratt County stone cutter. They were devilish things to read, with words in a spidery German script, but they kept Uncle Jack and Aunt Tildy advised as to when the stone arrived from the quarry and how the carving was progressing. Mr. Henkensiepen had unloaded the huge chunks of limestone close beside the same shed on which he had notched Uncle Jack's height measurement. Later, he asked Uncle Jack to tell Aunt Tildy (as if she could not read for herself) that he had personally stepped off one hundred and seventy-five feet and could readily discern the boys from the girls.

Aunt Tildy said Uncle Jack was like a kid waiting for Christmas. Still, it takes a long time, even for a skilled craftsman, to hollow out a piece of solid stone to where it can accommodate a man's body. It was late fall when Dutch Henkensiepen's big mules pulled the heavy wagon containing the completed sarcophagus up in front of Uncle Jack's porch. He was welcome as the flowers in May, and Uncle Jack, right off, offered him a Mason jar of *Comanche County Succulent Sarcophagus Completion.*

Now as Uncle Jack rather delicately put it, "If Tildy was suffering from any doubt or skepticism concerning discerning the boy cherubim from the girl cherubim or the boy seraphim from the girl seraphim, her mind was immediately put at ease."

Dutch Henkensiepen was put up for the night on a pallet beside the kitchen range, and the next morning he and Uncle Jack built an inclined plane sort-of ramp from the wagon bed to the ground. Art was dispatched to fetch the three strapping Whelpley brothers—Otis, Cleatus and Rastus—to ask for their help, and by noon the "sculpture," for only that can it be called, was safely resting on the ground before the front porch.

But Otis, Cleatus, and Rastus, after working up a good sweat and doubtless desiring some recompense, declared it had been a long time since they had actually seen a sarcophagus in use. "Damn and hell," they said. "I can scarce remember how the danged things work!" They demanded a demonstration.

Aunt Tildy said Uncle Jack was just as eager as anyone else. While they passed around a jar of *Comanche County Sarcophagus Supplement,* he changed into his G.A.R. uniform and reappeared with his sword with the ivory hilt clanging against his leg.

Of course Aunt Tildy had snapped photos of the whole procedure with her Kodak. She had the grand arrival of the big mules and the wagon. She had the somewhat grand arrival of Otis, Cleatus and Rastus, and she had Uncle Jack, more resplendent in his uniform than anyone had a right to be.

Aunt Tildy was never one to hold a grudge, but she did see fit to observe that Uncle Jack was mighty careful to wipe his boots before climbing into that sarcophagus. She said he had clomped his muddy boots across her fresh-scrubbed floors a million times but weren't about to mud-up his fine new sarcophagus. That was all right. A house is a sort of transitory thing. A sarcophagus, done right, is *forever*.

Unfortunately, what should have been a glorious and triumphant moment turned out to be a disaster. Uncle Jack, with great dignity, climbed into that wonderful stone box, and Aunt Tildy placed a pillow beneath his head and a worse-for-the-lateness-of-the-season posy in his folded hands. The flaw was immediately apparent. Uncle Jack's knees stood far and above the rim of the sarcophagus, and short of sawing his legs off, the lid would not fit on in a million years.

What had happened was this: in hollowing out the sarcophagus Mr. Dutch Henkensiepen had tossed the spalls, the chips of stone, along the base of his shed. It was the same shed which had given him shade while carving, and it was the same shed on which Uncle Jack's height was recorded. So the level of the ground grew higher, and Uncle Jack's apparent height grew shorter.

Aunt Tildy said the Whelpley boys were convinced that if they placed the sarcophagus lid on top of Uncle Jack's knees the problem would take care of itself. Dutch Henkensiepen said that was a great idea, but Uncle Jack more-or-less said it was not a great idea, then removed himself from the sarcophagus with alacrity.

"Alacrity," I must in honesty tell you, is not the exact way Aunt Tildy described Uncle Jack's sarcophagul exodus, but out of respect for her memory, I will let it stand. In point of fact, I have never witnessed a cat having its butt scalded and would be loath to try to describe it.

"Freeman's Folly"—that's what the sarcophagus was most often called.

Uncle Jack maintained, "Any time you're the first person in your neighborhood to get a sarcophagus, you have to expect a certain amount of jealousy from the small-minded."

For a while Uncle Jack tried to claim that the unusable sarcophagus had been the personal bathtub of Mary Magdalene. Aunt Tildy tried to claim that good luck would come to anyone who rubbed its male appendages, but they found few believers. A few neighbor girls, apparently completely down on their luck, *did* seem to spend an inordinate amount of time by the sarcophagus.

One day a professional photographer came out from Coldwater and offered Uncle Jack immortal fame by being photographed in his sarcophagus. Without taking an undue amount of time to think it over, Uncle Jack made a counter offer, assuring the photographer immortal fame by being the first man to have a wide-angle box Graflex camera—complete with tripod and flash tray—jammed up his fundament.

The fellow, also without taking an undue amount of time for consideration or meditation replied, "No offense intended."

Uncle Jack magnanimously told him, "None taken."

I don't know how or when the lid got broken into three pieces. Eventually the sarcophagus filled with rain water and became a horse trough, the only one known in Comanche County sporting Cherubim and Seraphim and male appendages.

About eighteen months ago I wrote a monograph entitled "A Brief History of Sarcophagi in Comanche County" and mailed copies to the more important libraries around the state, but I have yet to receive any acknowledgment. I believe most of us fail to appreciate the limited amount of time librarians have for correspondence.

28

Lincoln Coosey

In my mind at least, Lincoln Coosey is kind of a ghost–like figure. He was often there in the stories Uncle Jack told, but I never met him because he lay amoldering in his grave long years before I was born.

Though I was never able to learn many facts concerning Uncle Jack's early life, certainly not to the extent that I could write a scholarly paper on the subject, Uncle Jack always claimed that Lincoln Coosey was as close to a father as he ever had. Depending on what mood he was in, Uncle Jack also claimed that Lincoln Coosey became his sort-of father either because Lincoln won him in a game of three card monte or because Lincoln had to take him after *losing* a game of three card monte to Uncle Jack's father, who was a borderline ne'er-do-well.

But wheresomever the truth may lie, Uncle Jack told us on one drowsy evening that the life of young Coosey had been a hard one, mostly because of his name.

When Mr. Abe Lincoln ran for his first term as President, there were about four people in Texas who voted for him, and one of them was Lincoln Coosey's father. Little did he know that in a very short time only a few preachers and some sweet old ladies in Texas would be polite enough to refer to the new President as "a nigger-stealing son-of-a-bitch." Most folks were more harsh in their judgment. So Lincoln Coosey caught hell from all sides for being named "Lincoln."

"He made a feeble attempt to convince people that he had been named for one of the fellows in the nursery rhyme (Lincoln, Blinken and Nod) who sailed off in a wooden shoe one night. But the good people of Texas did not buy that for one minute.

"It was possibly fortuitous or possibly not—depending on how you feel about Salvation Army music—that the new armory at Tyler, Texas was built on land adjacent to the Coosey holdings. Lincoln Coosey's father, 'The elder Coosey,' not to be confused with *his* father, 'Coosey the Elder,' sought and found employment manufacturing rifles, first for the state of Texas, and then for the Confederacy."

Uncle Jack shook his head in sad disbelief and told us that in the known history of the Coosey family, which included the elder Coosey, his father, Coosey the Elder, and Lincoln Coosey himself, there had never been a sign of larcenous blood.

"Nevertheless," Uncle Jack said, "Lincoln Coosey had

memories of his father emptying out his pockets at the end
of the work day and saying, 'Damn! How did this trigger
guard get into my pocket?' or, 'Land sakes! I seem to have
inadvertently brought home a lock plate, a sear, three barrel
bands and a nipple.'

"Now, odd as it may seem, the evening came when the
elder Coosey sat with all of these rifle parts before him on
the kitchen table and found that, with very little filing and
fitting, they came together. 'My soul and body,' he
exclaimed, 'Just looky!'

"At this point, Lincoln's grandfather, Coosey the Elder,
who was old and crazy as a peach orchard boar and cantankerous as Methuselah's left-handed sisters' brindle cow,
straightened in his rocker and declared, 'Let him be acceptable to his brethren, and let him dip his foot in oil.'
Whereupon he died. But no one noticed, because Coosey
the Elder was ever prone to rehearsing his death and
rehearsing his last words."

"Wait now. Just back up." Aunt Tildy interrupted, "If
nobody was noticing and nobody was paying any attention,
then how do we know that Coosey the Elder's last words
were about brethren and foot-in-oil-dipping?"

"I stand humbly corrected," Uncle Jack replied.

"I do like the part about the oil because I have dipped
my aching feet in warm goose grease to relieve the pain and
the misery," Aunt Tildy admitted.

Uncle Jack lowered his stubbled chin in acknowledgment. "Those words were the words gravened on his headstone *as* his last words, and I expect it behooves us to accept
them. I admit that I, perhaps, spoke rashly and hastily when
I told you nobody had noticed. Lincoln Coosey noticed, but
only in an absentminded sort of way and then mostly only

when it came time to engrave the words on the tombstone. But the fact remains—the all-consuming and all-encompassing fact remains—that Lincoln Coosey's father was 'amazed and appalled' to find a new rifle in his hands. He declared the weapon to be 'a gift from God.'

"And a gift from God it may have been, but either God or the elder Coosey had not screwed the nipple for the percussion cap securely into the barrel. At the first shot, it flew out backward and pierced his brain—'his,' meaning the elder Coosey's brain, not God's. God was about up to His fetlocks with running the world, and Tyler Armory rifles ranked pretty low on His list.

"Most likely," Uncle Jack said thoughtfully, "Tyler Armory rifles came somewhere lower than, 'Zebra: the diuretic problems thereof.'

"At any rate, according to Lincoln Coosey, God did not even hear of the incident until three days later when his father appeared at the Pearly Gate. And when God saw the elder Coosey with about half of his brains sagging out through his eye hole, He roared, 'What are you doing here, you rifle-stealing rascal?'"

If the elder Coosey made excuses or replied I never learned about it because Aunt Tildy raised her skirt about four inches and shouted, "I am about up to *my* fetlocks in bull hocky! Get on with the story!"

"In the end," Uncle Jack said, resuming the story, "when the undertaker and the banker and the lawyers had squeezed and pummeled the estate for all it was worth, young Lincoln walked away with only a Tyler Armory rifle with a blown nipple and a book, missing the last three pages, titled *How to Win at Three Card Monte.*"

In my mind's eye I can see Uncle Jack reach down and

grope for the cast iron "Naughty Lady" boot jack which was never far from his chair. The "Naughty Lady," lay with hands clasped behind her head and legs open wide. And though, as a boy, I sometimes examined her covertly and hopefully, I found no trace, no delicate reason, why she should feel the need to cover herself.

Uncle Jack struggled and groaned until his boot was off, then rubbed his foot through the used-to-be-white sock, caressing it as if it were the baby Jesus and his last hope for redemption.

Aunt Tildy performed her estimation of how a very patient person might behave while waiting for a story to continue, but it was plain that she had no talent for the job. "Get on with the shotgun," she finally commanded.

"Well," Uncle Jack finally said, "Lincoln drifted around after the war. He lived a sort of catch-as-catch-can existence as did a good many folks of the Southern persuasion when the Confederacy went down. Meanwhile, Coosey the Elder and the elder Coosey both lay amoldering in their graves. The writing on the headstone of Coosey the Elder read, 'Let him dip his foot in oil,' and the stone of the elder Coosey read, 'Died of a loose nipple through the brain, and of such is the Kingdom of Heaven.'

"Eventually, God—in His infinite, if perhaps question-able, wisdom—either allowed or ordained Lincoln Coosey to arrive in Enid, Oklahoma as drunk as O'Rileys step-mother. And when he arrived, he came poor as a church mouse, with only that old Tyler Texas rifle and the three card monte book with the last three pages missing, but not a farthing in his pocket."

"Now what," Aunt Tildy required, "exactly is a farthing? And why might one reasonably be expected to want one in one's pocket?"

Let me say, if you have not already assimilated the fact, that Aunt Tildy was the crown jewel in Uncle Jack's life. Goodness only knows what kind of rough and shoddy life his might have been had it not been for Aunt Tildy. She abraded away his rough, even dangerous, edges. I just guess Uncle Jack would rather have had his gizzard spitted and slowly roasted over a green-twig fire than hurt Aunt Tildy. However, sometimes, like this time, she just seemed to grab the bait even where no bait was intended.

Looking back, I'm not sure but maybe it was Uncle Jack's habit to grab *Aunt Tildy's* bait.

Howsome-ever, it was at times like this that Uncle Jack winked me the wink I thoroughly loved, which meant "Hold on boy, and keep a straight face."

"A farthing, my precious, if unenlightened bride," Uncle Jack told her, "is a sort of English persimmon. In point of fact," he elucidated, "a few years ago a group of Englishmen settled in north-central Kansas, bringing and planting farthing trees. Well, sir, they had more money than the Duke of Leicester but were dumber than St. Bridget's goat, bringing only male farthing trees. Understandably, the trees did not bear fruit, and the second winter those Englishmen almost starved because…"

"Now, whoa up there!" Aunt Tildy interrupted. "Just who or what is a Duke of Leicester? And are we to understand that he could just strut around all day and all night with his pockets stuffed with persimmons? And the poor Englishmen, who desperately wanted to have their pockets stuffed with persimmons, had no farthings? Is that what we're to understand?

"And also," Aunt Tildy continued, "I believe I would

like to have a few goats around this place. Just because St.
Bridget's goat was dumb does not mean *all* goats are dumb.
I would teach mine some good tricks! And I would buy a little cart for one of them to pull and a fine black leather har-
ness with little glitteries on it. But it occurs to me to wonder hows come a saint has the leisure to maintain a goat
farm. It has always been my understanding that saints spent
their time washing the feet of the poor and the lame and getting jabbed at with spears. Also I wonder, is having goats a
Roman Catholic pastime? I dang sure would not want the
Pope hanging around pestering my goats.

"And also, also," she continued, "I have been in Enid,
Oklahoma with nary a persimmon in my pocket and
enjoyed myself immensely. So why did Lincoln Coosey
feel so put upon and so down-trodden because he did not
have a danged persimmon in his pocket—which he could
have had if he had spent his money on persimmons instead
of booze?"

"Just—gol-dang it to hell, Tildy!" Uncle Jack said, "I
did not say Lincoln Coosey *wanted* a persimmon in his
pocket. I said he did not have a *farthing* in his pocket."

Aunt Tildy pulled on the face she used in church when
the offertory was announced. "Then I don't understand
what all the fuss is about," she said.

"The point is," Uncle Jack's voice had raised a notch.
"The one and only point you need to keep in mind, Tildy—
forget St. Bridget, forget persimmons, forget the goats and
the gol-dang Pope—the point is this: when Lincoln Coosey
arrived in Enid, Oklahoma, he ran smack onto a cadre of
Salvation Armyists."

"I love the bass drums," Aunt Tildy proclaimed. "I
guess if the Pope offered me my choice of a goat or a bass

drum, I would be hard put to decide."

I saw Uncle Jack's face sag ever so slightly.

"Well, see, that was the trouble. That particular group of the Salvation Army did not have a bass drum. And that is how Lincoln Coosey came to bring eternal salvation to the evilest man in Oklahoma."

"His name was Bart," Aunt Tildy interrupted. "Evil men are always named 'Bart.' The worst ones are called 'Black Bart.' The ones who are pretty bad but not too bad are usually called 'Dirty Bart.'"

Uncle Jack was probably the most adaptable man I ever saw. He gave his head a patient little nod and said, "Now, this Bart was the meanest son-of-a-bitch in Oklahoma, and he knew he was a mean son-of-a-bitch. One day when he was on the road to Damascus, which is a little south of Enid, he came upon a burning bush, and the burning bush spoke unto him saying, 'You are a mean son-of-a-bitch!'

"'I know I am,' old Bart said, and he pulled off his boots and stomped that burning bush into the ground barefoot.

"But, by and by, old Bart begin to mellow. In the secret-most depth of his heart a germ, a longing, began to grow. And in his liquor-addled brain he concluded that only a religion or sect which utilized a large bass drum would suffice to bring such a mean son-of-a-bitch as himself to the ever-loving feet of the Lord.

"General William Booth, the founder of the Salvation Army, was the very man for old Bart.

"Well, sir, it sometimes behooves us to consider the vagaries of life. On the same evening, two men found their way into Enid, Oklahoma. There was old Bart, filled with the hope for redemption, and Lincoln Coosey, filled with demon rum.

"They met on a street corner where the Salvation Army band was tooting and belching and squealing out 'Rock of Ages.'

"By his own account, Lincoln Coosey was enjoying the performance mightily. He had a fine, clear tenor voice and loved to join the hymn-singing, but his downfall was his inability to remember the words, so he had a tendency to improvise. He tended to promise repentant sinners lifestyles which were even less condoned by the church than the lifestyles they were already living. Lincoln Coosey's theology was immensely popular amongst sinners.

"But old Bart did not find solace in Lincoln Coosey's melodic promises. He had wandered 40 years in the wilderness searching for the Truth and the Light, and by some kind of epiphany, determined that Truth and Light was, by and large, only found when accompanied by a large bass drum.

"So Bart's throat was all clogged with wormwood and gall and his umbrage was rising because there was not a bass drum amongst this whole, damn carload of Salvation people. Oh, there was a drum, but it was a pitiful little insignificant specimen. And I reckon Bart understood that such a mean son-of-a-bitch as himself would find little hope for redemption aided only by a tenor-drum or a baritone-drum.

"At any rate, in a pique of disappointment and unchristian rage, Bart pointed his finger and bellowed out for all to hear: 'That is a piss-poor excuse for a bass drum!' And those were his penultimate words, because it was then that Lincoln Coosey's old Tyler Armory rifle inexplicably discharged, removing a portion of the left side of Bart's skull.

"Bart lived only long enough to apologize and admit that that little drum packed more of a wallop than he had expected, and so he was saved.

"Lincoln Coosey said he felt that Bart likely had more to say on the subject of drums, but the Salvation fellow who played the tenor horn stuffed the rotogravure section of a newspaper into Bart's mouth to quiet him, announcing that Bart was not the only son-of-a-bitch in Enid who needed saving.

"The horn player mumbled that the Army band still had a number of hymns to play, some of which were in E flat, a key which he found to be a bitch to do on the tenor horn."

We sat in silence, each pondering the confusion of coincidence and how it relates to life. I remember that evening pretty well. There were a few clouds but nothing threatening, and we had the usual light breeze from the south.

Finally, Aunt Tildy said, "Will there be anymore persimmons tonight?"

"No, Ma'am," Uncle Jack told her.

"Farthings?"

"No, Ma'am."

"Then I guess I'll go on to bed." At the screen door she turned back. "Tomorrow I believe I will buy a goat," she said.

29

The Sad Demise of Captain Jack O'Hare

I sit here this afternoon saddened by the realization that my writing is not really up to snuff. There is no continuity. My thoughts ramble back and forth over the years. I have notes, written mostly on unpaid bills—which are a joke because my creditors are not eager to risk getting snake-bit coming out here to the ranch to collect.

Be that as it may, I remember starting to tell about Captain Jack O'Hare and G.A.R. Post #1000, but I don't believe I ever finished. This writing would doubtless be done in a more professional manner had I not been removed from the University newspaper for trying to write the complete and honest account of how Emmot Pierce G'damned his mule up the lane. I was, thereby deprived of the chance to learn the rudiments of journalism. I cannot give you the average length of life of jackrabbits in Comanche County because I was also rudely expelled from the Veterinary Science Library for mentioning "bunny clap," and the doors of academia closed before me—tighter than a bull's butt in fly-time.

Jack O'Hare lived to a ripe old age. When he died, he simply died of old age. I enter that because it seems there was ugly talk that he died of bunny clap or something similar. Uncle Jack attributed that ugliness to the fact that, no matter what they tried, they could not wipe the grin off Jack O'Hare's face. As the neighbors filed past the little white coffin, they looked at one another with uplifted eyebrows, and Uncle Jack knew what they were thinking.

The neighbors knew about Jack O'Hare's problem. They also knew that Emmot Pierce was bleeding Uncle Jack dry for salves and balms until finally Uncle Jack presented the bad end of his Smith and Wesson to Emmot Pierce's bellybutton and requested the recipes for the medication. Like most men with a revolver pointed at their bellybuttons, Emmot Pierce proved to be the soul of amenability and told Uncle Jack that he only regretted not having thought of passing along the recipe himself.

Aunt Tildy proved as adept at boiling up potions and balms as she was at making soap. Among her effects I found a hand-written proposal for an advertisement: "Tildy's Fine Bunny Balm." Unfortunately when Aunt Tildy explained to the editor of *The Coldwater Talisman* just exactly what Bunny Balm was, explaining that it would bring relief equaling, if not surpassing, "Lydia Pinkham's Vegetable Compound," he refused to run the ad.

Thereupon Uncle Jack rode into town and explained what he would do to the editor if he did *not* run the ad. Whereupon, the editor called in the sheriff, who explained to Uncle Jack what *he* would do to Uncle Jack if he did.

Well, sir, it's sad to reflect on the needless pain and suffering incurred by the jackrabbits in Comanche and the surrounding counties because that ad was not run. In Christian charity I will assume that the editor of *The Coldwater Talisman* had an advanced degree and was therefore not responsible.

In the little old building which has seen service as chicken coop, Grand Army of the Republic Hall, gold-nugget-storage-area for the Emperor of China, and Battle of the Wilderness Museum, there are, to this day, several barrels of Bunny Balm. I do not keep the Balm for sentimental reasons. I keep it because the Environmental Protection Agency has wrapped the building in chains and locks and steel cables, bulldozed dirt nineteen feet high over it, wrapped yellow crime-scene tape around the whole area, and promised me eleven years of solitary confinement if I even think of trying to dispose of it myself.

Now, why in the hell would I want to do that? Its burblings and glurglings give sound to the otherwise silent evenings now that the blue vapors curling up from the Bunny Balm have killed all of the fleas, flies, and locusts within, I would guess, three miles.

It is my understanding that the government is outfitting a cave in New Mexico with furnaces, strainers, filters, radiation machines, and chimneys 411 feet high to deal with the Bunny Balm. Judas Priest, why do they think we have Oklahoma?

Even while Aunt Tildy's dream of wealth and fame died

aborning, Captain Jack frolicked amid the sage and the tumbleweeds, his prosthesis *clicking* and *clacking* and broadcasting out a message of joyous love even unto the southern edge of Hodgeman County. No one who knew him was surprised when he died with a grin on his face.

Oh, yes, as Grand Commander of G.A.R. Post #1000, Uncle Jack felt compelled to chastise the Captain. He threatened him with demerits and demotion—but did not mean a word of it. He explained to Aunt Tildy that it was not the Captain's fault.

Uncle Jack contended that he had inadvertently built into the Captain's double-spring-loaded cantilevered and articulated prosthesis a sound which female bunnies could not resist. For a while he tried to recreate that sound, figuring he could make a fortune. A number of nubile and delightful young land turtles and one disoriented raccoon showed up but, as with other family fortune-making ideas, it was not to be.

Aunt Tildy told me the facts of the Captain's passing because Uncle Jack could not speak of it. He blamed himself for not thinking ahead and having on hand a carved stone sarcophagus, with or without male appendages, although it was Aunt Tildy's opinion that one without would have been an insult to the Captain's memory. So Uncle Jack with tears running down his cheeks the whole time, built the coffin himself with the same cedar lumber used to make the double-spring-loaded, cantilevered, prosthesis.

It was a sad thing to hear. What was its provenance: that lumber, that tree? Aunt Tildy had no idea. I have spent many an hour rocking and pondering and considering how the same tree could be used to give a three-legged bunny the mobility of a four-legged bunny—the élan and sex appeal, the downright sauciness, of a five or six-legged bunny—and then be used to build a sweet-smelling, mothproof, coffin. Boxed up—nailed down! The Captain. Judas Priest!

In my mind there nags a question of ethics. In my mind there nags, there nags—something that's not quite right.

Howsome-ever, the neighbors came, most of them were in debt to Uncle Jack and dast not come. The editor of *The Coldwater Talisman* did not show up nor send a representative to cover the event, so Uncle Jack spent many a pleasant evening jotting down thoughts and plans to cause the most lingering painful demise of that gol-danged editor. Uncle Jack never, absolutely never, mentioned that fellow's name or position without using that adjective.

Aunt Tildy told me there was no doubt about it, Captain Jack O'Hare's funeral was the largest funeral ever held in Comanche County. The few remaining members of the Official and *legally-sanctioned* local G.A.R. Post showed up because Uncle Jack had threatened to "cut off their water," if they did not. And even though most of them had either cisterns or deep-dug wells, whatever Uncle Jack had in mind was most likely not anything they would prefer to have cut off. So the vote was unanimous to attend the funeral.

They came in uniform, those of them which could still poke their stiff old limbs into the appropriate openings. One veteran carried an old snare drum even though the rawhide snares were long rotted away, broken and gone. The snares were of no matter because the drumsticks lay, long amoldering in their grave—at Shiloh or the Battle of Wilson's Creek or the Battle of Somebody's Ferry.

The ex-bugler carried his old bugle, and when Uncle Jack requested he play a solemn and dignified tribute to

Captain Jack O'Hare, he told Uncle Jack that he would be pleased and honored to, but he had lost the mouthpiece to the dang bugle while fishing for catfish.

Uncle Jack, who was admittedly a little testy at the time, asked "What in the hell does the mouthpiece of a bugle have to do with fishing for catfish?"

That old veteran scratched himself thoughtfully, grinned a grin which should have been left ungrinned under the circumstances, and said to Uncle Jack, "I just guess you have not had a great lot of experience catfish fishing."

Whereupon Uncle Jack, in no mood for foolishness, explained that he guessed the veteran had not a tremendous amount of experience in having the barrel of a .45 Smith and Wesson shoved up his fundament. Whereupon the veteran asked of Uncle Jack if he had a preference for the solemn and dignified tribute to be played in E flat or B flat, then scooted off behind the shed to practice his horn.

Uncle Jack had searched through the pile of cracked and scratched records and finally chosen John Philip Sousa's band playing "The Stars and Stripes Forever" to be played while bearing the remains to their finial resting place.

Little Lucy was placed in the back yard and given the serious responsibility of cranking the Victorola and manipulating the needle back to the start, time and time again.

To the best of my knowledge no one, not even Uncle Jack, held it against Little Lucy that she overrode Uncle Jack's choice and played her own favorite, "Keep My Skillet Good and Greasy All the Time." Folks in Comanche County were a lot more used to seeing rabbits in a greasy skillet than being carried in a white coffin by a fellow in an ill-fitting G.A.R. uniform with an ivory-hilted sword tripping him at every third step.

It was Aunt Tildy's personal and well-considered opinion that John the Baptist himself, on his best day, could not have delivered a more fitting eulogy nor a more stirring and inspirational sermon than did Uncle Jack. It is a credit to her honesty that she also admitted that John the Baptist, on his best day, was most likely not as full of *Bunny Burial Balm* as was Uncle Jack.

At any rate, the old veteran bugler, having determined to do his best to placate Uncle Jack and avoid any intimate relationship with a .45 Smith and Wesson, bugled a solemn and dignified tribute in *both* E flat and B flat without benefit of a mouthpiece, then died the next day of a ruptured aorta.

And thus was Captain Jack O'Hare laid to rest.

Wait, I must make a correction. It was not *Captain* Jack O'Hare who was laid to rest. It was *Major* Jack O'Hare. Uncle Jack, on the spur of the moment, gave him a posthumous promotion. Aunt Tildy said she figured the rabbit would have been made a General, or at least a Colonel, if Uncle Jack had not been too drunk to remember what came after Major.

No matter. The rank of Major was gravened on Jack O'Hare's tombstone.

It had seemed right and proper at the time, but as the months passed, and as Uncle Jack rocked and pondered and mourned, Aunt Tildy told me he seemed more and more morose and dissatisfied. By spring he had contracted to have another stone erected beside the first, an addendum, promoting Jack O'Hare to Seven Star General, with Oak Leaves, Laurel Leaves, carrots, ribbons and a representation of a jar of Bunny Balm, all surrounding the official Grand Army of the Republic symbol: an eagle gripping an

American flag which supports a fine star.

It occurs to me only now—now that I am too old to go tramping around looking, to wonder if ever another bunny in Comanche County has been so honored as to have an addendum added to his tombstone. Perhaps someone, some-time, pursuing an advanced degree in a Kansas Land Grant College will also wonder.

30

The Truth About the Civil War

Uncle Jack did not hold written accounts of the Civil War in high esteem, especially those concerning the Battle of the Wilderness—in which he was so intimately involved.

He complained that the history books had it wrong. Just all gol-dang wrong! He, personally, had talked with many, many, many of the old veterans from both sides, and they declared it was all a bunch of hooey. "Privies," they said. "The whole damn war was about privies."

This came as a great revelation to me, but the more I thought about it, the more sense it made. During my first year at the University I took notes as Uncle Jack reminisced about that war. I am grateful that I was there to record his thoughts which would otherwise have been blown away like the leaves of autumn!

To his credit, Uncle Jack did not let the fact that his nativity occurred the same year the war ended interfere with his memory of the war.

What word do I want? Hubris? Hubrisosity? Little matter, I remember with pride, fondness and bitterness the title of the paper I submitted to the department of history. "Jack Freeman's Theory Concerning the Strategic Importance of Privies During the Late Civil War."

"It is a story untold," Uncle Jack explained, "how many of those old battles started for the possession of an outhouse. The sad fact is that neither the Union nor the Confederacy had the foresight to provide an adequate number of privies."

Aunt Tildy rolled her eyes upward without missing a pea in the pod she was shelling. I opened my mouth, and she plugged one in, dead center. Together we were like a smooth-oiled machine. I expect that summer there was not a boy in the United States nor the majority of the Sandwich Islands more adept at catching raw peas in his mouth than I.

"Now, these days there is a great deal of talk about the question of state's rights and the freeing of the slaves," Uncle Jack explained. "And, doubtless those factors were important in the beginning."

Uncle Jack was ignoring Aunt Tildy and me. It was not that he lacked the sensitivity and refinement to appreciate pea-plugging into the mouth of a boy. Maybe tomorrow that would be his focus, and anyone desiring to discuss the Civil War would get nothing but a cold stare or worse, a wound from a .45 Smith and Wesson bullet in a place where the scar would not show.

"But if you reflect and consider," Uncle Jack said, "that you have thousands and thousands of men marching around. Sooner or later they are bound to say, 'Gol-dang, I do (or do not) believe that states have the right to secede from the Union,' or 'Gol-dang, I wish them slaves did not have to suffer under the lash, but the truth is, I need to whiz in the worst way, and them sons-a-bitches are most certainly hogging the privy.'

"See," Uncle Jack told us, (he was a born educator), "you take a Frenchman, for instance—which is not far removed from an amoeba. It matters not a whit to a Frenchman if he pees in a privy or against an oak or a Lombard Poplar. And it matters not a whit to a Frenchman, when he gets the call, if the Fifth Brigade of Napoleon's Personal Fusiliers and the complete alto section from St. Angelino's School for Girls is marching by. Your average Frenchman will not spend a great deal of time searching for a privy. Whereas American boys…"

Aunt Tildy was appalled by this. She cast me a hard look and said, "Max, did you ever pee on a whit?"

"No, Ma'am," I told her. I jumped because my personal habits were rarely questioned, and most likely she noticed that little jump and assumed that, if the truth were known, there were damn few whits which got past me without being peed on.

"I always take my foot and sort of scrape the leaves away first to make sure," I told her. Aunt Tildy jerked a nod of approval.

It is my belief that Aunt Tildy, like Uncle Jack, was always a little skeptical about the quality of my upbringing. She undoubtedly harbored a secret concern that when I was at home, I and my brothers and sisters were allowed, if not encouraged, to pee on whits.

Uncle Jack's face was growing red as it often did when Aunt Tildy sorted the gristle from the gravy in his stories.

"There is, in reality, no such thing as a gol-dang whit! The word 'whit' is what we use when we want to signify 'next to nothing.' If you need to dwell on it, consider this: a whit is 3/64 of an inch smaller than a 'nepotism.'"

It was evident from the tilt of her superior chin that Aunt Tildy now found herself on familiar and comfortable ground. "My daddy, back in Iway, had four hives of whits and one very large grove of nepotisms, so kindly don't presume to tell *me* what to pee on!"

"Judas Priest," Uncle Jack said. "Judas Gol-dang Priest. I am trying my level best to educate the boy as to his heritage and the history of our nation, and you keep dragging red-herrings across my path."

Aunt Tildy's lips parted, and I would bet the farm that she was about to ask me if I had ever peed on a herring. But Uncle Jack shot her such a cold and severe look that her lips closed.

"Now, The Battle of Bingham's Privy is a case in point," he said. With his finger he drew invisible battle lines on the porch floor. "You see, McClellan was marching his army down from the north, and old Jubal Early was bringing his army up from the south. They had both sent scouts out ahead, and both sides had espied the privy and recognized its strategic value. They were both determined to take it at all costs. Captains and lieutenants in both armies were galloping up and down the lines shouting, 'Hold on, boys, just a little longer.'

"In Jasperson's *History of the Civil War,* you can read about a twenty-year-old private in the 17th regiment from

Tennessee who said, 'Gol-dang, Lieutenant, I just don't believe I can wait.' And he didn't, because he couldn't, and so he was put up against a stone wall and shot as an encouragement to his associates to capture Bingham's privy.

"McClellan's third brigade was the first to appear over the cusp of Devil's Ridge, and five of Jubal Early's best sharpshooters, who had drank a great deal of cool spring water the night before, emerged at the mouth of Devil's Gap at a rapid trot and…"

"Now, wait, wait, wait!" Aunt Tildy told him. "What is all this Devil stuff? Devil this and Devil that! You are just making that up!"

"No, Ma'am! I am not. Just read your history. Any civil war battle worth its salt has got to have a passel of Devil things in it. Should you ever care to enlighten yourself, read Grimbledge's *Thoughts and Procedures Concerning Civil Wars*."

Aunt Tildy blinked her rapid, her impressed blink. "And just where might one reasonably expect to find old Grimbledge's thoughts?"

"In all honesty, I don't know. The only copy I ever saw belonged to Lincoln Coosey, and it was washed away in the flood of '93. But, rest assured, if you do not have a passel of Devil places in it, you are going to have a very disappointing civil war."

Aunt Tildy seemed impressed but not satisfied. "Well, I don't see why there can't be some Angel places too."

Uncle Jack seemed pleased with her mental acuteness and explained. "In 1804, in the state of Maryland, some folks tried to do a civil war, and they came together at a place called 'Angel's Paradise.' On the first day one fellow got his toe blown off and, as often happens in a civil war, neither the toe on the left of it nor the toe on the right of it were touched. So the next day the warring parties held a parlay and renamed the place 'Devil's Run.' By grab, in less than one hour seven men were killed and a goat had one of his horns blown off."

"I hate it when goats get hurt," Aunt Tildy complained.

"It's a cry and a shame," Uncle Jack agreed. "And if they had only named the place Devil's Run in the first place, the slaughter would likely have been only seven men and one toe."

"It ain't right," Aunt Tildy muttered.

Uncle Jack reached out with his gnarled and veiny hand and patted her knee. "There, there," he told her. Uncle Jack had his tender side.

Uncle Jack continued his story. "Old man Bingham had built the privy with his own hands, built it of stone and solid oak timbers, built it with the comfort and security of long generations of yet unborn Binghams in mind. Then, on the day of the battle he looked out over his meal of fried squirrel and oatmeal and said, 'Here they come, Mother. Damn, but I do get tired of civil wars!'"

Aunt Tildy was not so easily distracted. "Frankly," she said, "I prefer stories about goats over stories about privies. What happened to the goat?"

Through unconscious practice, as with a tic, or through inherited traits from unknown ancestors, Uncle Jack had the knack to draw the left side of his mouth towards his left ear while the right side of his mouth remained as calm, as placid, as unconcerned, as an old man sitting in front of his cabin whittling on a piece of mountain laurel.

It was a disconcerting sight. He did this mostly when vexed and exasperated, which was mostly when Aunt Tildy was interrupting his stories.

"The goat," Uncle Jack mused. "Well—well—then—the Gol-danged goat was rescued by a huge ship with golden sails and carried away to the south of France where it was married to an English princess who had wandered off the path while picking gooseberries!"

Aunt Tildy nodded her head and smiled. "That's nice," she said. "Goats are as good as anyone else, and I hate to see them always get the short end of the stick. What happened to the fellow who shot off his horn?"

"He was blown away like the leaves of autumn," Uncle Jack told her.

Once again he continued the story. "Now, Jubal Early had been expecting to fight in the mountains, so he had only brought along some fine mountain howitzers. Unfortunately, except for Devils Ridge which was only two feet and two inches high, the nearest mountain was about 23 miles away, and the cannon would only point nearly straight up—which any fool can understand would be a problem. So when old Jubal Early observed McClellan's third brigade marching nearer and nearer, he gave the order to fire. Those almost-straight-up-pointing cannon fired a ball that did not come anywhere *near* McClellan's army, but blew the complete chimney off Bingman's privy."

"All right, now wait." Aunt Tildy told him. "Just stop!" Her eyes closed as she carefully ciphered and calculated. "Not once during the many times nature has called out to me while the Fifth Brigade of Napoleon's Personal Fussilandros and the whole and complete alto section of St. Who-the-heck-ever marched by, have I ever found myself in a privy with a chimney!"

It did not bother me at the time. Only in my dottering

old age has this occurred to me: Uncle Jack could have had McClellan's army marching up and down the Shenandoah Valley doing double back-flips and singing "What a Friend we Have in Jesus." He could have had Jubal Early eating Grapenuts from a left-handed, silver-plated double-edged colander. He could have had U.S. Grant doing pirouettes in a tutu through the streets of Macon, Georgia in high-top brogans, and Abraham Lincoln importing the Fifty-Second Highlanders to play "Amazing Grace" on the bagpipes on a march through Tuscaloosa, Alabama. It would not matter a whit to Aunt Tildy. But, put a chimney on a privy, and look out!

"Well, there was a chimney on *this* privy," Uncle Jack flat out told her. There was a chimney because, besides having built the dang thing out of stone and oak timbers, Mr. Bingham had also built a chimney and put in a small, pot-bellied stove."

"Did this Bingham fellow keep any goats?" Aunt Tildy asked.

"Goats? Did he keep goats? Yes, Ma'am, he did." Uncle Jack sighed deeply. "All right. He had seven goats, two black ones, one spotted one, three white ones, and one who dressed like a gol-dang Arab who went around telling folks he was Ali Babba and asking had anyone seen his forty thieves! ...Now, would it be a great inconvenience to you if I got on with the Civil War?"

"No inconvenience whatsoever," Aunt Tildy replied. "I wish *I* had a goat."

"So when McClellan saw the carnage wreaked by those mountain howitzers, he called up his light cavalry and told them to get down there into Devil's Gap and stop the Rebs before they messed up the privy for everybody. Well, sir, it was a fearsome battle. The streams ran red with blood, and it was said you could walk across the whole battlefield stepping only on bodies and never once touch the ground. Men on both sides were blown away like the leaves of autumn.

"They got there, though, those light cavalry boys. But it was too late. One of those rebel cannoneers had chunked a dead log under the back part of his cannon and lowered the muzzle until, out of pure cussedness, it was aimed dead at that splendid three-hole accommodation.

"Stones and timbers flew all asunder, and the pot-belly stove was rendered forever useless and became a sorry shambles of its former glory."

"And what was Mr. Bingham doing all this time?" Aunt Tildy needed to know.

"It's almost to sad to tell." Uncle Jack told us. "As he ran out of his house waving his arms and shouting for everybody to get the hell away from his privy, one of his toes was blown off. He was a lucky fellow though, this being a civil war, the toes to the left and right of it received not a scratch."

"I'm sorry about that fine privy," Aunt Tildy said mournfully.

Uncle Jack thoughtfully ran his finger down his nose. Then pronounced, "War is hell!"

Young though I was when I heard those words, I realized they were profound and important. I underlined them three times in the paper I submitted to the history department. My professor pulled me aside and explained that those were *not* the words of any Mr. Jack Freeman! I braced *that* smart son-of-a-bitch tight against the tile wall and told him that I found it exceedingly odd that he, who was not there, seemed to know more about it than I did, when I was the one who was there listening and eating raw peas!

As Uncle Jack said, this is "a story untold."—except, I guess, for these few paltry words. Most of those old blue and gray boys are amoldering in their graves, and the true and full history of the American Civil War has been blown away like the leaves of autumn.

31

Aunt Tildy and the One-Wire Arapaho

I suppose I do not need to tell you that the stories Uncle Jack related on those summer evenings made a deep impression on me. But I am going to tell you anyway because that is a privilege of my years. I am indebted to him, mostly, for such education as I have—modified, yes, by Aunt Tildy's observations. Aunt Tildy had a way of cutting through the gristle and getting to the gravy.

I drove over to Coldwater a few days ago and heard a little girl say, "Wow, that's spooky!" For some reason that made me think of Aunt Tildy. Goodness knows I do think of her often, but I certainly don't think of her as "spooky."

Howsome-ever, Aunt Tildy did have her ways. Well,

Uncle Jack had told me she was 1/16 part witch, and I knew from firsthand experience that most everything she cooked tasted like turnips. Uncle Jack had said that was the major problem with being 1/16 part witch. He had drawn his finger down alongside his nose when he told me that, so I know it was the truth.

I have known a few folks besides Aunt Tildy who seemed to have special powers, but I was never much interested in delving into the occult. As I may have mentioned, my thrust has always been toward historical accuracy.

Neither do I for a moment believe in ghosts nor haunts, but I do not flaunt my disbelief loudly enough to offend any ghosts who might be lurking nearby.

Uncle Jack sometimes hinted at Aunt Tildy's *power*, and I could have learned so much—but I was mostly too dumb to ask questions. Also (I had just as well admit it) when I did ask questions, *they* were dumb too.

Uncle Jack told me once that Aunt Tildy had been born with a veil over her face. I guessed that meant she had certain powers denied to the majority of the rabble of this earth. Uncle Jack said Aunt Tildy could heal mysterious illnesses and also had the gift of prophecy. He said if Aunt Tildy were to be locked in a stone storm cellar, she could *prophesy* her way out in less than eighteen minutes. I always took Uncle Jack's words at face value, and I'm not about to stop now, but I will tell you on my own recognizance that anyone wishing to try to lock Aunt Tildy in a stone storm cellar without her consent had just as well not look to *me* for help.

In my opinion, there are numerous considerations more important than evaluating an old lady's prophetic abilities. Right up there among them would be not having your earlobe chewed off and not having your gall bladder dislocated to the point where it would making sitting uncomfortable.

Be that as it may, I went to Aunt Tildy and asked to see her veil. She gave me a strange look, but I was young and had grown used to receiving strange looks, so paid little heed.

Aunt Tildy was patience personified. She dried her hands on her apron, went to the closet, and dragged out her old veil. It was made of lace, all curlicued and delicate and covered with an applique of tulips and Rose-of-Sharon. By that time I knew enough about men and women and the miracle of birth to just stand in open-mouthed amazement. How in the world could a mother get that thing to stay on a baby's face while so much else was happening to distract her thoughts?

Whenever Uncle Jack got into the mood to speak of strange happenings and special *powers,* he always told about Sees Forever, the one Indian he liked and respected.

Like most boys I was fascinated by the American Indian. I knew they had lived and hunted and fought and loved right here where the ranch is, and sometimes, especially at night, it seemed I honestly could feel their presence. In my later life I have become diametrically opposed to Uncle Jack's feelings concerning Indians. But his point of view came from a different time.

Lord, just think of it, a whole different world!

And while I can't agree with his feelings, neither can I begrudge him his point of view. I sometimes asked Uncle Jack to tell me about the Indians, but he seemed to believe there was not much to tell: "Drunkards, beggars," was all he said about them. Except, that is, for the old, club-footed Arapaho named Sees Forever.

Sees Forever was apparently another of those people born with special powers. Whether or not he had been born with a black lace veil with curlicues and an applique of tulips and Rose-of-Sharon over his face I have no way of knowing. But he had an uncanny gift of sight. Uncle Jack said Sees Forever could often see things even if they were not there, and even when he was sober.

Sees Forever had a length of copper wire which followed on the ground behind him. That was part of his "Strong Medicine."

God only knows where it was attached to the basic Arapaho, hidden somewhere under his clothes. Uncle Jack claimed it was a "Medicine Wire," and that Indians always had about them a "medicine this or a medicine that." He said that if all the other Indians had found out about how much good medicine Sees Forever absorbed from that copper wire, the telephone and telegraph would have never survived in Comanche County.

I think I have mentioned that Uncle Jack was an odd mixture when it came to what we call "progress." He could not abide the telephone, but he did embrace the concept of electricity. He read every scientific book or magazine which came his way if it was about electricity, and he was convinced that it took two wires to make a circuit. He told me one wire bent around to *resemble* two wires and attached to the "juice" was a serious mistake because you can not fool electricity. At any rate, my Uncle Jack was a smart old man and if he could not have received an advanced degree in Electrical Engineering from any university in this land I would be very much surprised. He said an Indian such as old Sees Forever with only one wire, would, most likely, be lacking in the realm of wattage, amps and ohms.

Ohms, Uncle Jack told me, had to do with resistance, and Sees Forever did not have an appreciable amount of that.

"And temptation," Uncle Jack said, "can only be resisted if one has the required ohms in regard to the temptation at hand which needs resisting. The word 'ohms' is an abbreviation for 'Oatmeal, Ham, Mincemeat and Sauer-kraut.' If you eat enough of those, you will be able to resist damn near anything."

I attribute my own moral failures, which may or may not include fathering a child or two over in Barber County, to my inability to get the first forkful of sauerkraut down my gullet. On the other hand, I eat a bowl of oatmeal every morning for breakfast and have never in my life stolen a horse. I don't know how to account for the German fellow who lived north of here who ate sauerkraut morning, noon and night. Yet every maiden's father in Kiowa County had a shotgun shell with the name "Ginderstadt" written on it.

"As for mincemeat," Uncle Jack said, "You give an Indian a plate full of mincemeat, and he will dump it on the ground and stomp on it and curse you and your progeny into six generations. So whether he is a one-wire Indian or a two-wire Indian he is mostly likely suffering the want of a couple of ohms."

Uncle Jack would be the first to admit he had little or no education in the field of commingling between Arapahos and hoot owls, but anything Sees Forever could see in the daylight he could see just as well at night. And when he saw it, he sometimes gave out with a "*Who-whoop-a-woo.*"

Uncle Jack said it was one of life's mysteries.

Not even Uncle Jack knew exactly where Sees Forever lived. He came and went like a nebulous spirit. Even Uncle

Jack never knew exactly when Sees Forever would show up. He almost always showed up when Uncle Jack was in need of help, and sometimes he showed up even before Uncle Jack realized he needed help.

That's the way it was on the day when Uncle Jack rode over a ridge and found Sees Forever lying all sprawled on the ground where he had been mending Uncle Jack's fence. Sees Forever lay with a bullet crease along the side of his head and a stranger standing over him muttering about "stinking Indians."

Now this, you understand, was a way back before Uncle Jack's soul had the calmness and serenity it later achieved. And so Uncle Jack, without any adieu at all, and without even inquiring as to where the remains should be sent—on the off chance there happened to be any—pulled his Smith and Wesson, and in the youthful exuberance so prevalent in that day but so lacking in the youth of today, blew away enough of the cartilage from the stranger's throat area as to make "keeping his chin up" an endeavor with which the stranger no longer need concern himself.

Uncle Jack blamed the slightly-off-the-mark, slightly-gone-astray shot on emotional weakness and offered it as an example of what can happen to a fellow when he grows too fond of an Indian. But it did the job, and I have always considered it a mark of Uncle Jack's innate self-forgiving nature that he did not dwell on that poor shot.

Sees Forever was still alive, but his wound had made him as blind as three pounds of bacon. Uncle Jack picked him up like a baby, carried him right inside the house, and laid him on his and Tildy's own bed.

At first Aunt Tildy was outraged because some of her people back in Iowa had not found Indians to be as receptive to the advancement and glories of civilization as had been anticipated. But then her healing and nurturing nature took over. She gathered her balms and herbs into the bedroom and closed the door.

After the first day's ministrations, Aunt Tildy whispered through the slightly cracked-open door that Sees Forever was now only as blind as two pounds of bacon, and Uncle Jack knew everything would be all right. He said the odor of turnips in that room was so strong it would have been instantly fatal to people not born with veils on their faces. Aunt Tildy asked Uncle Jack to procure a small bowl of dried and pulverized larkspur root and a shot glass of essence of hollyhock, then to simmer the whole thing over a slow fire for 18 minutes. She also asked for a pint of turtle fat. When Uncle Jack asked if she could use rattlesnake fat instead, Aunt Tildy bristled, "That's the trouble with you men! You think anything in the world can be resolved with rattlesnakes."

Uncle Jack confided to me that he did not take any offense because such was often the response from a professional when an unlicensed practitioner makes the mistake of trying to be of a little help.

Aunt Tildy kept the windows shut and the curtains closed, and Uncle Jack said he heard some mighty strange mutterings coming out of that bedroom. Occasionally there was a bellow from the Indian or a shriek from Aunt Tildy, by which he knew they were both still alive.

But by and by, about the end of the second day, she opened the door another crack and said that the "damned Indian" kept squirming around. During the night the head poultice had slipped clear to the foot of the bed. She told Uncle Jack that the Arapaho's sight had not improved, but his club-foot was completely healed.

On the third day Aunt Tildy came out of the bedroom looking tired and wilted. Sees Forever was now only as blind as one pound of bacon, but the effort was taking a great toll on Aunt Tildy. Her hair was unkempt, which was not like Aunt Tildy at all, and her eyes squinted as if she were trying to see something far and away.

Long about suppertime Aunt Tildy appeared again, this time with Sees Forever trailing, but not limping, behind her. Sees Forever stepped out on the front porch looking a mere shadow of his former self, which Uncle Jack said was not that much at look at in the first place. He shaded his eyes with his hand even though the sun was mostly down and peered into the distance. "I see four fence posts down way out on the north fence," he announced.

Late as it was, Uncle Jack saddled up old Dobbin and rode over to inspect the north fence. Well, sir, there were only three fence posts down, so Uncle Jack rode home with the intent of killing the "lying son-of-a-bitching Indian."

But Aunt Tildy explained to him that she had worn herself to a frazzle healing old Sees Forever, and if that Indian got shot again, she was through with the whole mess. She said he just need not bother to bring home anymore shot Indians.

The next day Sees Forever appeared restless and eager to be gone, but first he and Uncle Jack sat on the front porch to smoke a pipe together in friendship and muse over the past few days. That old Indian had been blind and now could see. He had been club-footed and now could dance a hornpipe was he of a mind to.

In the interest of cultural observation, I asked Uncle Jack if the Indian had shown any inclination whatsoever to dance a hornpipe, and he told me, "No."

Sees Forever was in complete and worshipful awe of Aunt Tildy. He considered her a powerful medicine woman. Uncle Jack figured Sees Forever, had it been requested of him, would have stayed there forever as her personal slave. But I guess Aunt Tildy had had about enough of Indians to fulfill her requirements, so she presented him with a croker sack of turnips and an admonishment to eat one every day until he could tell the difference, at a distance, between three fence posts and four fence posts—so as to prevent being shot by Uncle Jack.

They watched together from the front porch as old Sees Forever lit out for parts unknown, trailing his copper wire, neither knowing nor caring if he had enough ohms to see him through the day. Uncle Jack, having nothing better to do, idly followed Sees Forever as far as the top of the ridge. He told me when that old Indian believed he was out of sight, he threw the croker sack of turnips on the ground and used his two good feet to stomp the bejesus out of them. It was Uncle Jack's considered opinion that a man with two good feet could put them to no better purpose.

32

The Gentle Side of Uncle Jack

It bothers me, on reflection, that I may have presented Uncle Jack as a violent person. He was not. He did shoot a few people, but they were mostly miscreants and sons-of-bitches who needed shooting, and we must bear in mind that there were more people Uncle Jack did *not* shoot than those he *did* shoot. There were also those he shot, but not very hard.

No, I remember Uncle Jack as a soft-hearted man who would spend hours whittling a prosthesis for a three-legged bunny. I remember him as the man who brought art to Comanche County in the form of a sarcophagus/horse trough sporting cherubim and seraphim with male appendages.

If not everyone in Comanche County appreciated Uncle Jack's cultural contribution, it was most likely because they were either miscreants or the other thing, and understandably, could not be expected to have an appreciation for art.

Now that I think of it, there was a fellow down from one of the more northern counties of Kansas who examined the horse trough and declared it to be of the Italian style. He said that Leonardo de Vinci would likely have made one just like it, if he had thought of it.

That pleased Uncle Jack immensely because he was a great admirer of Leonardo. He said Leonardo invented damn near everything worth inventing except the .45 Smith and Wesson and doubtless would have done that had he lived longer.

Uncle Jack said it was a cry and a shame that de Vinci did not invent the .45 Smith and Wesson because the Italian countryside was alive with miscreants and sons-of-bitches and could certainly have used it.

Still, Uncle Jack was of the liberal-minded persuasion and would have been the first to tell you that in the realm of miscreants and sons-of-bitches, the Italians could not hold a candle to the French. But when all was said and done, both the French and the Italians, right along with the Oklahomans, were a part of the lost tribe of Israel who had likely wandered away from camp in the middle of the night to take a leak and been too dumb to find their way back.

I have found no historical reference to this at all, but Uncle Jack was convinced. And no one who ever saw the horse trough could deny the male appendages.

If Aunt Tildy were here today, she would back my claim that Uncle Jack was one of the most gentle men who ever lived. She always smiled her loving, gentle smile when she told the story about the boisterous galoot and the fly. It showed Uncle Jack's soft side and his good will toward all of God's creatures.

It seems that one day, through no fault of his own, Uncle Jack accidentally found himself in a saloon in Coldwater. He was sitting at a quiet corner table discussing the social and economic benefits of the iron plow in Chowan County, North Carolina with the undertaker, old Deafy Himmelspiegle. Deafy was as deaf as a horseshoe, and for that reason, believed they were discussing a Sunday School teacher he had tried to seduce in Weehawken, New Jersey in 1888.

Aunt Tildy said it was a mark of Uncle Jack's patience and accommodating nature that he was in the midst of turning the discussion in the direction of the social and economic benefits of using an iron plow to seduce Sunday School teachers when the problem arose.

I should tell you, if I have not already, that Aunt Tildy was a woman of great wisdom and understanding. She understood, for instance, that it takes a good deal of lubrication to accommodate a discussion of either iron plows or the seduction of Sunday School teachers. And if you tried to mix them together, you were likely to leave the meeting well-lubricated indeed. It was Aunt Tildy's pride that Uncle Jack was equal to the task.

At any rate, a loud and boisterous galoot had caught a fly between his two hands. Holding it aloft, he announced its fate to the assemblage: "I shall pull its wings off and eat what-the-hell-ever is left over, for I am a miscreant and a son-of-a-bitch!"

Uncle Jack stood, gently slid his chair aside, and loosened the fit of his Smith and Wesson in its holster.

"Old son," Uncle Jack quietly explained to the galoot,

"it is my considered opinion that in the eyes of God, one of His creatures is about equal with any other of His creatures. We are admonished in the book of *Galatatans* 1:056.30: 'Let him who wisheth to have his own God-damn wings pulled off by Saint Smith and Saint Wesson be the first to pull the wings off that fly.'"

At first the room was filled with hoots and guffaws. But as the gentlemen witnessed the dark cloud which covered Uncle Jack's face, the hoots and the guffaws sort of melded into "Amens" and "I'll take my oath on that!"

Aunt Tildy said that while she had some reservations in the realm of Lincoln Coosey, she had to give him credit for instilling in Uncle Jack the ability to explain the Bible in a manner which the average layman could understand.

Well, this good old boy either did not understand or else underestimated the power of the "word" to an unfortunate degree. Without a hint of sympathy or remorse, he proceeded to pull off the left wing of the fly.

"An eye for an eye, a tooth for a tooth, and a wing for a gol-dang wing! Book of Escalations 90:5465," Uncle Jack proclaimed in his quiet and peace-loving manner. He then proceeded to plug the fellow in his left arm, although, not as accurately as one might have hoped. As before mentioned, it was one of Uncle Jack's more endearing qualities that he never chastised himself for making poor shots.

Doubtless benumbed by demon rum, the loud and boisterous galoot was still able to use his left hand well enough to pull the right wing off the fly.

Aunt Tildy said Uncle Jack was understandably perplexed by a man who could ignore both the word of the Good Book and a .45 Smith and Wesson, but he rose to the occasion.

"A wing for a wing," Uncle Jack repeated, "and another wing for another wing," then plugged him through the right arm. The fly was obviously dying and in horrible and miserable pain, so Uncle Jack picked it up and stuck it up the fellow's nose as an example of an Example. He then likely found a little time on his hands, and started to enjoy his afternoon. He plugged the galoot's nose holes with a portion of hard boiled egg which the galoot had bought and paid for, but which lay neglected and uneaten because of the excitement of pulling the wings off the fly.

It was Aunt Tildy's opinion that probably about the same time the editor of *The Coldwater Talisman* was setting the galleys of type, once again portraying Uncle Jack as a cold-blooded killer, Uncle Jack was having a serious, if one-sided conversation with the County Coroner. The result was that the death certificate read: "Death from *"Hard-Boiled-eggus in Nostrilites."*

I expect that loss of blood could have also been listed as a contributing factor, but death by loss of blood happened every day in Comanche County. To their credit, our citizens have always appreciated a little variety on their death certificates.

What it comes down to is this: if you needed shooting, Uncle Jack would oblige you. If you needed being carried home to the Freeman place, laid in his own bed, and nursed back to health, Uncle Jack would oblige you. If you needed a dose of culture which might include cherubim and seraphim and male appendages, then Uncle Jack was your man of the hour.

In Comanche County, the most humble, insignificant, and unable to protect themselves—be it fish, fowl, insect or any other thing which creepeth on the face of the earth—

could sleep in peace knowing that the gentle man of peace, Jack Freeman, was there for them.

Without a doubt, the miscreants and sons-of-bitches of Comanche County squirmed and tossed in their miserable beds, dreading the morrow.

33

Aunt Tildy Remembers an Albatross

Now, where was I? Oh, yes, I want to tell about the albatross. I believe it must have been autumn because I seem to see more owls in autumn than at any other time of year, and I do enjoy hearing them *whoop*.

One night an owl flew over the porch. I believe it was before World War II, although it might have been shortly after.

But now that I think about it, it was around the start of the war. I was being loaned out to Uncle Jack and Aunt Tildy for a few days because I had accidentally burned down my father's barn, and he seemed to need a vacation.

At any rate, that was the time when Uncle Jack, who was nearly 80, rode to Coldwater to volunteer as a paratrooper and was laughed out of town by the Selective Service Board.

This board had the authority to determine a man's fitness for duty on a scale of "1-A" to "4-F." They gave Uncle Jack a personalized rating of "12-Q," which brought them closer to death than they ever knew.

Uncle Jack came home red of neck and fierce of eye to retrieve his .45 Smith and Wesson and go back and kill every son-of-a-bitch in Coldwater. But Aunt Tildy told him he likely did not have enough bullets to do that. When Uncle Jack turned to pick up his weapon, she cold-conked him with what she claimed was a fossilized sweet potato.

Lord, sometimes I think I should have gone into philosophy rather than history. I expect a lifetime of pondering could be done just considering the ramifications of how one fossilized sweet potato changed the whole history of Coldwater, Kansas.

When he came to, Uncle Jack announced that he had now been wounded in *two* wars and had given about all which was in his strength to give for his country. The subject of enlisting in the paratroops never surfaced again.

So, as I started to tell, one evening this old owl flew over the porch. Uncle Jack smiled and pondered and considered the fact of owls. He was very fond of owls. Had he ever met one who needed a prosthesis, you would have found Uncle Jack at the head of the line to build it.

On this evening I'm telling about, the wind was scouring the earth and sending most of the good topsoil far and away toward Junction City. Dark, black, sin-laden clouds seemed to be filled with chicken feathers, owl feathers, dried skunk droppings, and tumbleweeds. They sort of swirled and twirled past the porch.

Uncle Jack looked at me woefully and said, "In the Pleistocene period, what the owls ate, mostly, was young boys."

Gol-dang, I did not take it as a personal favor when Uncle Jack preambled his evening story with a phrase like that!

He told me that he had once found the fossil of an owl with the fossil of a small boy in its belly. He said he had tossed it into the well with the rest of his fossils because, inexplicably, "That fool George Sternberg was not in the least interested in it."

If I wanted to see it, however, he promised to tie a rope around me and lower me down the well when the weather cleared up.

"Bull Hocky!" Aunt Tildy told him. "You stop trying to scare the boy. Frankly, I am sick and tired of hearing about how wise owls are. They are culturally deprived and morally depraved."

"'Morally depraved?' Owls? Morally depraved? In truth," Uncle Jack said, "it surprises me to hear you say that. Why, Lincoln Coosey had a picture of St. Cecile with an owl on each shoulder and... "

Aunt Tildy puffed up and told him flat out: "Lincoln Coosey may well have danced the quadrille with an owl up his nose! And Saint Cecile may have had owls nested in both armpits and three more in a croker bag, but that does not prove them *praved*."

Uncle Jack stomped into the house and came back with his dictionary. He ran his finger down line after line. "There is no such gol-dang word as '*praved*,'" he told her.

Aunt Tildy did not have what we would nowadays consider a first class education, but she was a woman who lived in harmony and closeness with the earth. She understood

the use of herbs, roots and balms and had the power of healing. Sometimes, it seemed to me, she could cause things to
happen which, rightly, should not have happened. But it was
a grave mistake to tell Aunt Tildy any thing or anybody
could be *de*praved had they not previously been *praved*.

I expect even William Jennings Bryan would have died
of apoplexy had he tried to debate with Aunt Tildy on
whether or not a man could become *de*ranged ere he had
been previously *ranged*. Neither could a purchase be
*re*turned without first being *turned*.

But Aunt Tildy was plainly not in a mood to speak of,
nor be spoken to, on the subject of owls.

She had discovered Samuel Taylor Coleridge's *The
Rime of The Ancient Mariner* somewhere and brought out a
well-worn copy.

"Well," she announced, "*you* may be in a mood to
discuss owls, but *I* am in a mood to discuss albatrosses."

Uncle Jack, flushed with the victory of believing he had
proved one could be *de*praved without having been previously *praved*, appeared to be ready to challenge the existence of the albatross.

"Don't bother," she told him. "I am from Iway, and in
Iway you can't walk to the privy without stumbling over 16
or 17 dad-blamed albatrosses.

"There was a fellow who lived south of us, Bart was his
name…"

Now it was Uncle Jack who interupted, "Would that be
the 'Black Bart' I've heard you mention?"

"No, sir, Aunt Tildy told him. "This fellow was
'Previous Bart' because he was named after his father who
was named 'Black Bart'. In that family they were too tough
to ever use the name 'Junior.' Anyway, being Roman

Catholic, they liked the Latiny-sound of 'Previous.'

"And see," Aunt Tildy continued, "I can understand their line of reasoning because if you think about it, 'previous' sort of means 'aforementioned,' but it would be a cry and a shame to name a boy 'Aforementioned.'

"Now Previous Bart fathered another 'Black Bart,' who proved unworthy of the name, and so got hauled into court where his name was legally changed to 'Irvine.' But the blot on the family escutcheon was too much for old Previous to bear, so he went out to the coal shed to hang himself.

"Well, sir, the fact of it is this: the old fellow plain did not bathe; he smelled so poorly that the first three ropes he tried broke in disgust, and he lived to the age of 79."

"For the love of sweet, limping Jesus, Tildy," Uncle Jack broke in. "What in the hell are you talking about?"

"Well, sir, if I might be granted an exemption from rude and blasphemous interruptions," she told him, "I would be talking about albatrossi, their domestication and their cultural attainments."

Uncle Jack lowered his head, acknowledging the rebuke and giving his oath that, barring personal implosion, he would withhold further comment.

"By hook or by crook," Aunt Tildy continued, "most likely it was by crook, Previous Bart acquired an albatross. Although most folks believed Previous' major talent lay in the field of mail-train robbery, through great patience and gentleness, he taught the albatross to play 'Au Clair de la Lune' on the tenor banjo."

It was then I noticed that Uncle Jack might indeed implode. More likely, he might explode, and I figured if he did, his "Bull Hocky" would be heard in the capital city.

"But, odd as it may seem," Aunt Tildy told us, "the folks

in Iway did not take kindly to having an albatross play 'Au Clair de la Lune' on the tenor banjo. At every county fair and at every church social, there was that danged albatross hammering away on his banjo. I figure it made them feel insecure and inadequate, which by and large they *were*.

"Perhaps surprisingly, at that time, a large percentage of folks in Iway could not, themselves, play 'Au Clair de la Lune' on the tenor banjo."

Uncle Jack broke his oath of silence long enough to explain his belief that at this point there were precious few things he might hear which would surprise him.

"So the whole nasty mess was taken to court, and the judge explained to Previous Bart that he would either have to make that damned albatross stop playing the tenor banjo or else the albatross would be hung around his neck. Furthermore, Previous and his descendants would have to wear it unto the twelfth generation.

"That was acceptable to Previous Bart because he was partial to the tenor banjo, but the albatross resisted with all his might because Previous Bart did not bathe and smelled like... "

"Judas Priest!" Uncle Jack exploded.

"That's right!" Aunt Tildy admitted, "He smelled just like Judas Priest."

Uncle Jack stomped off to bed.

I said, "Aunt Tildy, no bull hocky now. Did that albatross really and honestly play the tenor banjo?"

Aunt Tildy looked at her lap for a while and then grinned at me, "He did, but I'll tell you something which I would never say in front of your uncle. That old albatross was not as smart as I made him sound. Previous Bart had to tune it for him."

34

Lincoln Coosey and the
Soft-Shell Oklahoman

In our evening stories death was a subject to which
Uncle Jack and Aunt Tildy seemed drawn. It was by no
means an obsession with either of them. I don't want to
leave that impression. It's just that there comes a time in our
lives when the realization hits us that on the highway of life,
we are approaching the edge of the map. I suppose by the
time I was spending my summers in Comanche County,
both Uncle Jack and Aunt Tildy must have felt they were
about in the Seward County (the third-from-the-edge of the
Kansas map) part of their lives.

I have recently noticed a trend, especially at funerals,
wherein folks proclaim that "death is a part of life." I take

issue with that. Either they don't understand life or I don't understand death. Had I the time remaining to me to organize my thoughts—which I do not (because I am in the Morton County part of my life)—I would write a learned paper on the subject.

In those far away Comanche County summers, death held little meaning for me. Death, in itself, was not as frightening as the stories which that dad-gummed Uncle Jack liked to tell just before bedtime. At bedtime he liked to tell about the fellow who had hanged himself, and by the time he was found, his neck had stretched out to about three feet long.

More usual were stories like the one Aunt Tildy told about the little boy back in Iowa who was forced by his step-mother to work in an organ factory and lay, for days, being slowly crushed to death by an organ-making machine. She said he had screamed and screamed in absolute and profound agony, but the workers around him were testing an organ pipe for tone and did not recognize the sound. They mistakenly thought the pipe was pitched wrong, and so kept cutting it shorter and shorter. By the time the poor boy was discovered, it was too late—the pipe had been ruined.

One evening when Uncle Jack was reminiscing about old Lincoln Coosey, he got off on the story about the soft-shelled Oklahoman.

"I was down in the Oklahoma Panhandle one time," he began. "I had not wanted to go, not in any way, shape, nor form. But Lincoln Coosey wrote and said he was lonesome to see me. Old Lincoln had been mighty good to me when I was just a sprat, and I figured I owed him that much. So I gathered together what few possessions I owned and turned Old Dobbin towards that accursed land.

"Well, sir, when I arrived I found that Lincoln Coosey had not become as frail as he had led me to believe, but I was mighty glad to see him anyhow.

"Now, this was in the little town of Wheeless, which is on the western edge of the Panhandle. It was about the most deplorable excuse for a town I have ever seen, but Lincoln had found a job on a hard-scrabble ranch and seemed to be settled in there.

"It happened we were in line awaiting our turn at a prominent business establishment when Lincoln Coosey noticed a poster which had been nailed to the side of the building. It announced an exhibition of unicycle riding to be held the following day. The show was to be put on by two brothers, and could be seen for a few pennies.

"Now, wait, just wait," Aunt Tildy said. "The prominent business establishment was a dad-gum whorehouse, wasn't it?"

Uncle Jack considered and pondered as to a response which might save his neck.

"I just hated to be there. It was a terrible embarrassment for me. But you know how Lincoln Coosey was about women, especially blond women with massive thighs. His favorite, he claimed, had a tattoo of Admiral Dewey when he was still just a midshipman."

"You must remember," he continued quickly, "that this was about 1885, and the wheel had only just been introduced into Oklahoma. In point of fact, the wheel on Orville and Wilbur's unicycle may well have been the only one in Oklahoma at that time."

"Lord, Lord," Aunt Tildy put in, "I did not know the Wright Brothers came from Oklahoma!"

"No, Ma'am," Uncle Jack said, "I doubt they did. These

fellows, these particular Orville and Wilburs, were named *Smith*."

"Were they the two black-beards who invented the cough drop then?" Aunt Tildy needed to know.

"No, Ma'am," Uncle Jack said again. "It was a different Smith family. Orville and Wilbur never met the cough drop fellows. But there is no reason to believe that *had* they met, they would have been less than the best of friends.

"However it was not fated to be. Young Wilbur was destined to die the next day."

"Now, I'm sorry to hear that!" Aunt Tildy exclaimed. "I hope there were no goats damaged in the explosion."

"Tildy, Tildy, there were no goats damaged, and there was no explosion."

"Thank you, Jesus," Aunt Tildy commented.

Uncle Jack relit his pipe, which had gone out during the confusion concerning Wrights, Smiths, goats and cough drops.

"Lincoln Coosey was a man with a scientific mind," he told us. "While the majority of Oklahomans at that time either did not believe in the existence of the wheel, considered it to be a passing fad, or a downright work of the Devil and an affront to Christianity, old Lincoln seemed to believe it had a future. He was not such a fool as to think there would not be problems—'likely a few kinks to work out' was the way he put it. But he was determined we should go and see the unicycle exhibition for ourselves and thereby have a basis on which to judge the future of the wheel.

"Orville Smith was the eldest and appeared to be the dominant brother. Although they had both worked in the construction of the unicycle, it was Orville and Orville alone who was allowed to ride it. Wilbur seemed to be a cocky little fellow, and doubtless Orville believed that unicycle-riding was not for someone with a frivolous nature.

"So when folks had paid their pennies and the tent was full, out came Orville, wheeling the unicycle, with Wilbur trailing along behind him looking like a muskrat which had learned to walk on its hind legs.

"Orville was a chunky and pretentious-looking man, lacking humor in his visage. Wilbur was small and wiry and, like I said, sported a sort of rodent-like face; he was not a man to be trusted. Doubtless old Orville should have known better, but while he adjusted his suspenders in preparation for the ride, he handed the unicycle to Wilbur to hold. With every eye in that tent upon him, it was too much for Wilbur to pass up his one chance for glory. Quick as a cat he sprang onto that unicycle, and in less than thirty seconds, he was dead as Kelsey's nuts."

It was Uncle Jack's contention that there are two types of Oklahoman: *specie* and *sub-specie*."

"The *specie* constitutes the majority of Oklahomans, and that would be your Hard Shell variety. Their skulls are so thick and hard that a fellow could crack black walnuts on them without waking them from a nap. Contrariwise, the *sub-specie*, or Soft Shells, have skulls so thin they break asunder at the slightest thump."

As with most things concerning Oklahomans, Uncle Jack made little pretense of understanding this phenomenon. "Oklahomans are just Oklahomans," is what Uncle Jack said. "The phrase 'leave hope behind all ye who enter here,' should be applied when trying to understand Oklahomans.

"It was just Wilbur's fate and bad luck to be born of the Soft Shell persuasion," Uncle Jack told us. "There was no way of knowing it beforehand of course. Finding out if an

Oklahoman is a Soft Shell is akin to finding out if a girl is a virgin—by the time you know for sure, it's too late. That old unicycle flipped over backwards and Wilbur's head cracked like a pumpkin. End of the story.

"To prevent a lynching, which would only have made Orville's day worse than it had already become, the admission price was refunded, although most folks seemed to think they had gotten their money's worth.

"Well, sir, Lincoln Coosey did a complete reversal of opinion concerning the future of the wheel. He said, 'Them damn things had better be outlawed before the whole human race is wiped out!' I understand that there were a few attempts by the Oklahoma Legislature to do that, but they came to naught."

We sat, the three of us, rocking, and pondering the sad fate of Wilbur Smith, the Soft Shelled Oklahoman. By and by Aunt Tildy spoke up. "Reminds me of the fellow back in Iway who died with his head in a barrel of pickle brine."

Uncle Jack mulled that over for a while and inquired, "Would you say, and I realize you have been away from Iowa many years, that death by pickle barrel is a common way for Iowans to die?"

"No, sir, by and large I would say that, considering the hard winters, fewer people die with their heads in barrels of pickle brine than one might expect. But Jacob Hendrix did. He was a pickle maker by trade, and by all accounts he rarely wore a gold locket."

Uncle Jack and I exchanged glances, and Uncle Jack cautiously advanced the opinion that that was likely a point in Jacob Hendrix's favor.

"Well, sir, one morning his wife came into the bedroom and found him rummaging through the bureau drawer. She said, 'What in the world are you doing rummaging through that bureau drawer?'

"He told her he was rummaging through the bureau drawer because he was looking for his mama's old gold locket.

"Whereupon she told him that she hoped to goodness he would find it and throw it away. 'That thing is bad luck,' she told him. 'You know your mama was wearing that thing on the day she died from cat-scratch fever.'

"'Bad luck is a superstition of the ignorant!' Jacob retorted. And to prove his point, like any man would do, he hung that locket around his neck when he found it and went out to check his pickles.

"Well, sir, lunch time came and lunch time passed, and she figured he had ruined his appetite by sampling his wares again. So off she stomped, down to the picklery..."

"Picklery?" Uncle Jack questioned.

"Picklery!" Aunt Tildy of-coursed. "And *who* do you think she found with his head in a barrel of pickle brine and dead with his mama's locket around his neck?"

"Well, Judas Priest, Tildy, we have no idea," Uncle Jack said. "Was it Bill Grigsby? Was it Tom Flanagan? Was it..."

"Not a one of them," Aunt Tildy said proudly. "It was old Jacob Hendrix, and he was dead as Kelsey's nuts, and his mama's gold locket had turned all green."

Uncle Jack shook his head from side to side in near disbelief, then said, "That is a cry and a shame."

"It is," Aunt Tildy admitted. "It is. All those years they had thought it was gold, but it was only brass."

"So whatever happened to the picklery?" Uncle Jack reasonably inquired.

"Belly up," Aunt Tildy told him. "It plain went belly up.

No one could remember *which* pickle barrel they had found his head in, and the possibility that a dead man wearing a green locket had spent several hours staring at the pickle they were about to eat was just too much."

So there we sat again, pondering the many ways folks die. Finally Aunt Tildy announced, "I have never been able to make good pickles. I doubt you've noticed, but it seems to me that my pickles always taste a little turnipy."

"Why, no," Uncle Jack lied through his teeth, "I never noticed."

35

Sad Farewells

Death, as it must come to us all, came finally to Uncle Jack and Aunt Tildy. Uncle Jack was near 90 when he passed, and no one on God's green earth knew the age of Aunt Tildy when she passed. She never told her age. No one dared ask.

Both died peacefully in their beds with assistance from neither unicycle nor pickle barrel.

Uncle Jack was not buried in his G.A.R. uniform. Aunt Tildy could not abide the thought of him lying there all those years in that tight, uncomfortable thing. He *was* buried with the ivory-hilt sword. And Aunt Tildy tucked his G.A.R. medal into the vest pocket of his old blue suit—which was likely a misdemeanor.

Aunt Tildy chose a coffin I considered too plain by far for Uncle Jack. It sported not one cherubim, not one seraphim, not one male appendage. The old sarcophagus lay half sunken in the front yard with its lid long ago broken in three places.

Aunt Tildy died a few months after Uncle Jack. I was with her and heard her last words: "I did all I could."

I reckon she did.

The emptiness in my life caused by their passing is beyond my power to describe; apparently I am not yet so old nor so tough as to be able to prevent these tears.

It occurs to me that I have scarcely mentioned Uncle Jack and Aunt Tildy's children. They were all mostly gone from home by the time I started spending my summers at the ranch. The only one of the four of them I ever really knew was Charlie.

Charlie, whom some historians credit with establishing the first marshmallow delivery route in Comanche County, died a fat but wealthy man at the age of 52.

Their oldest boy, Art, died at the age of nineteen because he swallowed his tongue. I found a copy of his death certificate in the Courthouse at Coldwater, and the cause of death was listed as "Lingus Swallowus." It was doubtless written by someone with an advanced degree.

Ben, the second son—and the first dead person I ever saw—tripped on a whiffletree when he was 43 years of age, striking his head. And, for the short bit of life remaining to him, he refused to wear anything but a smile. I have talked to folks who saw Ben in those last few months. To a man, they said, "Yep, it's hard to forget old Ben's smile."

The whiffletree was not damaged and was later sold to

Ralph Converse up on North Fifth Street. His wife said he did not need a damn whiffletree, so he told her to go to hell, which, many believe she ultimately did.

"Little Lucy," who was no longer little, was killed in Numerous, Idaho. She was run over by a stage coach during the "Territorial Days" which happened to be commemorating the death of a woman in Numerous, Idaho who had been run over by a stage coach.

Because Uncle Jack and Aunt Tildy's children had all died untimely deaths, I inherited the ranch.

I haven't kept any cattle around for several years. Frankly, I am too busy selling rattlesnake venom. There's an outfit in Chicago which buys all I can provide.

A fellow came out a while back and told me I had the finest venom there was. He thought I should change the name—that *Aunt Tildy's Fine Fang Fixin's* lacked the marketing panache needed in today's business world.

I rubbed my hand down along Uncle Jack's tied-down Smith and Wesson. "Bull hocky," I told him, "Bull hocky."

photo: Max at the Sternberg Museum, Hays, KS

Fish-Within-A-Fish

ABOUT THE AUTHOR
Max Yoho

Born in 1934 in Colony, Kansas, Max grew up in small towns. Moving with his family to Atchison at age 10, he soon learned that delights and adventures along the Missouri River awaited just outside the well-oiled hinges of his bedroom window screen.

Max graduated from Topeka High School and attended Washburn University in Topeka, where he was a feature writer for *The Washburn Review.*

After a thirty-eight year career as a machinist, Max retired in 1992 to begin a new career as a writer. With a number of poems, short stories, and one novel, ***The Revival***, previously published, ***Tales From Comanche County*** promises more belly laughs.

From the studios
of Books In Motion